THE
PRESENT TAKERS

Melanie Prosser and her gang had the school sewn up. Round behind the cycle sheds, every time it was another girl's birthday, they had ways of getting what they wanted – and the ways hurt.

Lucy and Angus knew they had to crack Melanie's system. It wouldn't be easy; in fact it would be horrible. But they knew the whole class was behind them.

Aidan Chambers

THE PRESENT TAKERS

A Magnet Book

First published 1983 by The Bodley Head Ltd
This Magnet edition published 1985
by Methuen Children's Books Ltd
11 New Fetter Lane, London EC4P 4EE
Reprinted 1986
Copyright © 1983 Aidan Chambers
Reproduced, printed and bound in Great Britain by
Hazell Watson & Viney Limited,
Member of the BPCC Group,
Aylesbury, Bucks

ISBN 0 416 51000 0

1

LUCY BEWARE MELANIE PROSSER
SHE IS OUT TO GET YOU Angus x x x

How do you know? And stop sending me notes.

I HERD x x x Angus

"Wait here," Melanie Prosser said at the school gate. "Then we won't miss her."

"In her daddy's posh car," Sally-Ann Simpson said. "Showoff pig."

"I'll put an armlock on her," Vicky Farrant said. "I'm amazing at armlocks."

"Not till we've got her behind the cycle shed," Melanie said. "Be all smarmy smiles till then."

From the corner of the school hall Angus Burns watched the three girls hanging about by the gate.

He knew they'd wait for her today, being her birthday. Just like Prosser to think of that. He also knew what he would like to do to Prosser: kick her fat teeth in.

Angus swept the hair out of his face and scanned the road, the school field, and then the drive right up into what he could see of the playground, looking for Clare Tonks. They'd be giving her a day off today while they had a go at Lucy. Poor old Clare, all she ever got was days off when they were bored with her, and were giving themselves a change by tormenting somebody else.

Angus spotted Clare at last. He could hardly miss her if she was in sight, she was so big in every direction. Tonks the tank. She was standing inside the cycle shed just out of view of the gate, and watching Angus.

"A new pencil case will do for me first time," Sally-Ann said. "My old one is grotty."

"Could put a neat half-nelson on her," Vicky said. "With a wrist-lever to screw on the agony."

"Save something for another day," Melanie said, as patient as a granny.

"Or put her down with a hip throw, do a step-over toe hold, and really make the silly bitch scream."

Melanie yawned.

Sally-Ann giggled. "You and that wrestling. I reckon you're a bit loopy."

Lucy Hall came downstairs wearing her new blue birthday shoes. She could hear her father backing the car out of the garage.

"Is it such a good idea to wear those?" Sarah Hall said meeting Lucy at the door to say goodbye.

"Stop fussing, Mum." Lucy gathered her things into her school bag.

"Don't complain if they get scuffed."

"They won't."

Jack Hall blew the car horn.

"'Bye, Mum, see you this after."

They kissed before Lucy ran to the waiting car.

Last five weeks, Sarah thought, then the holidays and after that she goes to the High. Seems only yesterday she started at Infants. Where does it go?

She waved as the car drove off.

"Morning, Mrs Harris," Melanie said as the teacher hurried through the gate.

"Morning, girls," Mrs Harris called, stopping to look. "What are you doing here? Can't you play in the yard?"

"Lucy's birthday, miss," Melanie said, sweet as candy floss.

"Got a surprise for her," Sally-Ann said, simpering. She was good at simpering, because she thought she was right in every way to play Annie in the musical, and had practised a special simper so that she would be ready when the call came.

"I'd forgotten," Mrs Harris said. "And, heavens, isn't she on hamster duty today? I'd better see to them myself. Have you a nice surprise?"

"Smashing," Vicky said flatly, her eyes on the road.

"How thoughtful of you." Mrs Harris strode away up the drive.

"Old bat," Sally-Ann muttered.

"Shut it," Melanie said.

"Mrs Harris," Angus said, stepping into the teacher's path.

"Hello, Angus. Early for a change."

"Lucy's birthday."

"So I gather." Mrs Harris glanced back at the group by the gate. "She's popular all of a sudden."

"I thought—"

Mrs Harris waited. "Come on then, dear. I haven't all day."

"—I thought you might meet her."

"Meet her?"

"Her birthday and that."

"At the gate, you mean?" Mrs Harris laughed. "No, couldn't do that, Angus. I'd have to meet every one of you on your birthdays if I did. I'd never be done. Anyway, Melanie and Sally-Ann and, what's her name, Vicky Farrant are there with a surprise. We'll all sing 'Happy Birthday' after registration as usual, so the occasion will be properly celebrated, won't it? She isn't royalty after all."

"It's just—"

"Yes?"

Angus blushed. Or, at least, what little of him Mrs Harris could see blushed. His face was mostly hidden by his hair. Luxurious you might call it; long certainly.

Mrs Harris laughed again, louder this time. "Well, I never! You of all people, Angus Burns! A dark horse, you are. You've good taste though, I'll give you that."

She stepped around him, about to go inside leaving Angus staked to the spot with embarrassment; but stopped.

"There is something you can do that would help Lucy, and me as well, if you want."

Angus brushed the hair out of his eyes and managed to look at the teacher. "Miss?"

"Feed the hamsters. Lucy's meant to—"

"But, miss, I—"

"You'll see her later. And think how pleased she'll be."

Mrs Harris took Angus by the shoulder and drew him with her into school. Angus looked back furiously at the group by the gate as he went inside.

Jack Hall stopped the car a safe distance from the gate.

"Friends of yours?" he asked nodding in the direction of the three girls who had come out onto the pavement.

"Same class," Lucy said, busying herself unnecessarily with her bag.

"Pleased to see you from the way they're waving."

"Just being silly. 'Bye, Dad."

"Happy birthday again, sweetheart."

They leaned together and kissed, Lucy pulling away quickly and getting out.

"See you later," Jack said.

"'Bye." Lucy slammed the car door and watched her father drive away. She would rather he were out of sight before she faced Melanie. Till that moment she had pretended to herself that it wouldn't happen. Not to her.

(8)

But Melanie and the others came pelting towards her.

"Hi, Lucy!" Melanie called breathless with gush, grabbing Lucy's spare hand in what might have been a friendly grip if, looking on, you didn't know better. She gave Lucy an awkward hug.

Sally-Ann and Vicky frisked and stomped on either side. "Sure," they said. "Happy birthday!"

"Ten today!" Melanie said, an announcement to the world.

"Eleven, if you have to," Lucy said, trying to pull her hand away.

"*Eleven!*" Melanie's eyebrows rose and her grip tightened. "Isn't that great, everybody! Lucy's *eleven* today!"

Sally-Ann giggled.

Other children, passing by, gave them a wide berth.

"All growed up," Vicky said.

"Give us your bag, then." Sally-Ann snatched it. "I'll carry it for you today. What an honour!"

Lucy swung her hand to snatch her bag back, but found instead that her arm was grabbed by Vicky and twisted up behind her.

"Let me go!" she shouted, trying to wriggle free. She had heard people shouting like that before as the same thing was done to them, but she had never interfered, as nobody did now.

"Run!" Melanie ordered, and she and Vicky towed Lucy along the pavement, through the gates, and took her stumbling up the drive, across the playground, all unhindered, and round behind the cycle shed, where they were out of sight of the school building.

All the way Melanie and Vicky, and Sally-Ann bringing up the rear with Lucy's bag hugged to her like something precious, laughed and whooped.

★

From the classroom where he was feeding the hamsters Angus heard their noisy progress. He threw the rest of the food into the cage and dodged across the room to the windows overlooking the playground. He was just in time to spot tail-end Sally disappearing behind the shed.

Some of the other kids were watching, but no one was following. Angus searched for Clare Tonks, at first could not find her, then saw her shadow looming at the back of the shed, leaning against the wall. Only the bricks, Angus thought, were separating her from what was happening on the other side. She could probably hear every word Prosser and her goons were saying. He'd ask her later.

Angus turned from the window. Mrs Harris was paying no attention, busy with work at her desk.

"Can I go now, miss?"

"All done?"

"Think so."

"The fish?"

"Yes, miss," he lied. He'd see to them at break. They wouldn't die before. Lucy was more important.

"All right."

He sped away.

"We only want to *talk* to you," Melanie was saying.

Sally-Ann had thrown Lucy's bag at her feet. She and Vicky held Lucy's arms out, pinning them against the cycle shed wall. To avoid Melanie's eyes, Lucy stared across the field at the houses on the other side of the road.

"Want to hear all about the fabulous prezzies you got this morning," Sally-Ann said.

"Some fancy stuff, I bet," Vicky said, "your dad owning a shop and that."

Melanie nudged Lucy's bag with a foot. "What've you brought to show off?"

"Nothing!" Lucy's reply was a note too triumphant.

Melanie's face lost its grin. "Must have." She crouched

and slowly unzipped the bag, watching Lucy's face all the time.

Lucy forced herself to keep quiet.

"Best make sure," Sally-Ann said. "Don't mind, do you, Luce."

Melanie started rummaging.

Her temper fraying, Lucy could not help crying out, "Leave my things alone!"

"Shut up, Whining Winnie," Vicky Farrant said between clenched teeth, and gave Lucy's arm a sharp nip that made her catch her breath.

Running feet echoed round the shed. Angus burst into view, skidding to a stop at the corner. He glared at the little group frozen into statues by his arrival. But the hair closed over his face at once. Melanie stood up, glaring back. "Had an eyeful?" she said, hands on hips.

"Leave her alone," Angus said unimpressively.

"What's it to you, you hairy beanpole?" Sally-Ann said. She had a voice that sliced your ears when she wanted it to.

"Just leave her, that's all."

"He do fancy her," Vicky said, matter-of-fact.

"Oooo—d'you think so!" Sally-Ann hooted.

"No I don't!" Angus said too quickly.

"Yes you do," Melanie said, not even smiling. "Well, you needn't worry. We're only talking. No harm in *talking*, is there? So you can just bug off, Angus Burns, because what we're having with your *sweetheart*—" she paused, challenging him, "is a *private* conversation."

There was silence. Angus opened his mouth, then shut it. He looked sideways as if someone out of sight round the corner were talking to him.

"Have you got some of your stinky friends with you?" Sally-Ann shouted. "They don't scare us. You know what'll happen if we tell Mr Hunt you boys have been bothering us girls."

Angus shifted on his feet, looking back and away. Finally

he brushed the hair out of his face and said, "Just watch it, Prosser, that's all."

"I'd rather not watch your ugly mug at all, if you don't mind," Melanie said. "*Yuk!* Put your hair over it again!"

"I'm warning you," Angus said, straining against his anger.

"Don't forget old Hunt," Melanie said.

Angus hesitated; then, seething, slowly backed away round the shed corner.

As soon as he was gone, Melanie turned on Lucy. "Rotten friends you've got. No bottle."

"Not half as rotten as yours," Lucy said, unable to restrain herself. "And Angus Burns isn't my friend."

"Not good enough for you, eh?" Vicky said.

Sally-Ann said, "Never mind all that. What about the prezzies?"

"Nothing much in her bag, just the usual stuff," Melanie said, her eyes not moving from Lucy's. She had unsettling eyes, like a cat's, grey, and they didn't blink much.

"I told you!" Lucy said.

"Funny what you notice though," Melanie said, "when you get down to earth."

"What she on about?" Vicky said to Sally-Ann.

Sally-Ann looked down, and hooted, "Ooooo yes!"

"Eh?" Vicky said.

Melanie, her eyes still unblinkingly on Lucy's, pointed with a finger. "We'll have to teach Pukey Lukey some manners," she said. "No prezzies, but showoff new shoes."

"So she has!" Vicky said. Lucy felt the grip on her arm tighten.

"Happy birthday, Lukey," Melanie said, and, moving very close, pushed her lips, exaggeratedly wet and pursed, into Lucy's face. Lucy twisted her head to avoid the soggy kiss. Melanie's lips landed, squelching, on her ear.

Melanie stepped back. "All right, little Miss Stuckup,

we'll just have to show you what happens to people who won't be friendly."

"It shouldn't be bad *this* time," Sally-Ann said like a nurse comforting a patient before an operation.

"Ready," Melanie said.

Vicky and Sally-Ann each raised a foot above one of Lucy's.

"Stamp!" Melanie ordered.

The hovering feet pounded down onto Lucy's toes, screwed this way and that, and lifted off.

Lucy cried out, and instinctively tried to bend down to grasp her feet and comfort them. But Vicky and Sally-Ann pinned her against the wall; all she could do was squirm, and shift her feet about inside her shoes, trying to wiggle the hurt out of them. Tears filled her eyes. Through them, as she bent her head to hide her face, she saw the scuffed and dented surface of her birthday shoes.

She had been wanting them for weeks. Her father had made a special trip to Gloucester to buy them for her, and this morning, longing to wear them, she could not resist the temptation. Now the pain in her toes was nothing to the distress she felt for her ruined gift. She hated Melanie for that.

As soon as she recovered her breath and could see properly again, she glared her hatred at Melanie, who laughed, as if pleased by such passionate dislike.

"Come on, Pukey," Melanie said. "Tell us all about your other presents."

Lucy shook her head.

"You must have millions," Sally-Ann said. "Stuckups like you always do."

Lucy shook her head again, fighting herself to say nothing.

"Think you're something, you do," Vicky said. "Coming to school in that poncy car."

"Other people come in their parents' cars." She could not

help herself. Why should they get away with saying such stupid things about her?

"I don't," Vicky said, twisting Lucy's arm a turn.

"And not in showoff big ones like your dad's," Sally-Ann said.

"He has a big car for his work. He has to carry a lot."

"Work!" Vicky sneered. "Call what he do *work*. Owning a shop."

"Doesn't own it. He manages it."

"Same difference. Up the workers."

"What do you know, Farrant!"

"Here," Vicky said, "don't get fresh with me." And she banged her forehead against Lucy's.

Lucy's eyes swam again.

Vicky observed the results with close interest. "Head butt," she said. "Might make it my speciality."

Sally-Ann said, "Vicky's going to be a wrestler, aren't you, Vick?"

"As if we didn't know!" Lucy said.

"She watches it every Saturday on telly and even goes and sees them live when they're at the Leisure Centre, don't you, Vick? She's going to be the first woman champion of the world. Over the men as well as the women, of course. Aren't you, Vick?"

"As you've no prezzies with you," Melanie said, "you can invite us to your party tonight."

"Not having one," Lucy said, still battling her tears.

"Too mean," Vicky said.

"Having it in the holidays, if you must know." Lucy was furious at herself for letting them provoke her into telling them anything.

"Can't wait till the holidays," Melanie said. "You'd better bring me a present tomorrow to make up for it."

"Me as well," Sally-Ann said.

"And for Vicky," Melanie added.

"Something nice," Sally-Ann said. "Something lovely

and new." She placed a finger tip on the end of Lucy's runny nose and began pressing slowly.

"Like a squashed tomato," she said.

"You won't forget, will you, Lukey, dear?" Melanie said.

At that moment Mrs Harris came striding round the corner.

"Now, girls, what are you doing here?" she called.

Melanie stood back; the others let go; Lucy wiped at her face with the back of a stiffening hand.

"Nothing, Mrs Harris," Melanie said brightly. "Just a game. Lucy is a robot that's broken down and we're repairing her."

"Well, I'm sorry to spoil your fun, but you should be inside. You'll be late. Quickly."

Melanie snatched up Lucy's bag and ran off. Sally-Ann and Vicky grabbed Lucy's hands again and pulled her along with them. All friends together.

They let go as they entered the building and made for the cloakroom.

"Don't forget," Melanie said cheerfully, "see you tomorrow before school."

2

Mrs Harris led the class in singing "Happy Birthday". Lucy pretended to be pleased but was really too upset to care. One or two of her friends gave her cards, but more diffidently than they might have done, knowing what had just happened outside. Samantha Ling gave her a little brooch made of something that looked like red fruit gum with yellow Chinese writing on it.

"Your name," Sam said. "Hope you like it."

"It's pretty. Thanks, Sam." Lucy looked round to see if Melanie had noticed, but luckily she and Vicky and Sally-Ann had their heads together round their corner table. Plotting, Lucy thought.

Samantha said quietly, "What were they doing to you?"

Lucy, looking closely at Sam's present to avoid her eyes, said, "Nothing."

"They weren't getting onto you, were they?"

Lucy shook her head, though she couldn't think why she lied. "I don't want to talk about it."

"If they were, you should go straight to Mr Hunt."

Lucy kept quiet.

"You're not going to be friends, are you?"

"Course not."

"What was going on then?"

"Nothing."

Sam waited.

"Look," Lucy said, "I've told you. I don't want to talk about it, that's all." She turned away.

Samantha sniffed. "All right," she said, "be like that!" And she went off and made noisy conversation with Mary Gardiner, who, as usual, was busy organizing Mrs Harris.

Half way through the morning Angus came gangling over to Lucy.

"Borrow us a needle, Loo," he said, leaning his spiky elbows on her table and talking through his cascading hair.

"My name is Lucy, if you don't mind," Lucy said, not stopping her work.

"I've got some paper to stitch for that book we're making." He waited but got no reply. "I hate stitching."

Lucy said at last, "You should have brought your own needle."

Angus had a scrappy piece of paper held between his fingers. He dandled it between Lucy's eyes and her work.

"I had one," he said. "But I lost him."

"You would," Lucy said, pushing his dandling hand away with her pen. "Being stupid."

"Can't all be geniuses," Angus said, putting the piece of paper on the table and fiddling about with it. "Did the hamsters for you though, didn't I."

"The hamsters!" Lucy said, hand over mouth. "I clean forgot."

"Birthday present," Angus said, pleased. "Sort of anyway."

"Thanks," Lucy said but not sounding grateful. "I'll do it when it's your turn."

"Borrow us a needle, then." He flipped the piece of paper onto the page where she was writing.

Anything to get rid of him. "Here," she said, fishing one out from her bag. "Now go away."

Angus took the needle and ambled back to his place.

"Dropped her a note, I think," Sally-Ann whispered to Melanie, who made no move to look.

"One throat chop, he'd be out like a light," Vicky said. "He's a weed."

"Is she reading it?" Melanie asked, working away.

Sally-Ann bobbed up from her seat, pretending to ease her skirt. "Letting it lie."

"He's not that bad, I expect," Melanie said. "Under all that hair."

Sally-Ann leaned closer. "Don't fancy him, do you, Mel?"

Melanie looked up from her maths and winked.

Five minutes later Lucy could not help herself. She poked at the grubby scrap with her pen.

It had to be another of Angus's notes. She was half fed up, and half amused by them. He'd been giving her one every day for the last two weeks. The first she had discovered sticking out of one of her shoes when she got back from a games lesson. The second had been glued to the bottom of her pencil case with a piece of chewing gum. The third had been delivered to her home; written on the envelope in large red letters were the words: SECRET AND PRIVAT AND CONFIDENSHAL. There was no stamp so he must have brought it himself, either very early or late the night before.

But today's note—the tenth—was the only one he had almost handed to her. Must be getting brave, Lucy thought. Or desperate. And she had to admit that she was keen to know what this one said.

As casually as she could manage, she unfolded the scruffy page.

TODAY 1700 RAILWAY CROSSING
GOT PLAN 2 STOP PROSER
xxx Angus

Lucy smiled for the first time since arriving at school. All Angus's notes were attempts to get her to meet him, but were never subtle. PLEASE MEET ME AFTER

SCHOOL OUTSIDE GATE—that kind of message. One of them, the eighth, had begun U R THE GREATEST and was the first to finish with an x. Lucy thought them so funny she had kept them, safely tucked away in a small pocket inside her bag, so that she could read them and cheer herself up when she was bored.

Twice she had taken him at his word, and met him. The first time to satisfy her curiosity; the second, after his note about her being the greatest, because she took pity on him. Both times she went home afterwards wishing she hadn't bothered. Angus had done nothing but bumble about, paying her hardly any attention, and dragging her across muddy fields between school and Whiteshill. There he abandoned her outside his house with hardly a word. This was not Lucy's idea of a date.

Not that she had ever had a proper date. Melanie Prosser had, of course. Several, if what Sally-Ann said was true. All of them with much older boys from the High School, which all the other girls seemed to think was very daring. And judging by what Sally-Ann said happened, Lucy's meetings with Angus did not count as dates at all. They were just mucking about. Kids' stuff.

Lucy glanced across at Melanie's table and met Sally-Ann's eyes gazing back at her over the top of Melanie's bent head. Spying, as usual. Sally-Ann twinkled her fingers in a brazen wave.

Lucy looked away, and pushed Angus's note into her bag with the others.

What was all this 1700 nonsense and having a plan to stop Melanie? Was it just a dodge to get her to meet him again? And she wished he'd just forget about Prosser and what had happened this morning. She wished they all would; everybody would be talking about it. She hated the thought; the whole thing made her feel unclean. Small. A mutt. She couldn't find the right word.

And anyway, Prosser could eat Angus for breakfast and

still feel hungry. Angus. Aberdeen Angus. A kind of cattle they make steaks out of. Angus Steak Houses. She had seen them in London. Her father would not take her to eat there because he said he wanted fish and somewhere quieter.

Aberdeen Angus. A rather stupid bull. Hardly a bull yet, though, more like a skinny calf. A long streak of steakless stupidity. She found herself smiling again. But he was good for a laugh, and that was something.

Though you only had to look at him and then straightaway look at Melanie (who was still bent over her work, chewing the ends of her hair as she often did when she was trying to concentrate) and you could tell that Melanie knew about a thousand times more than Angus about everything to do with the hardest parts of life. Like making other people do what you wanted, and how to be nasty without really trying. They were both the same age and both in the same class, but Angus looked like a boy and mostly behaved like a boy, whereas Melanie—well, Melanie wasn't exactly a woman yet but you could tell she knew what it meant.

Not that she, Lucy, was any better than Angus. Beside Melanie she felt like a rake. She had hoped being eleven might make a difference. But of course it hadn't. And what Melanie had done this morning only made her feel more like a kid than ever. Some birthday present—being made to feel more childish just when you were wanting to feel grown up.

"What's this, Lucy?" Mrs Harris said, coming up from behind. "You don't seem to have done much."

"Thinking about my project, miss," Lucy said, pulling herself together.

"You look very glum for a birthday girl. Are you all right?"

Dragging energy from the pit of her stomach, Lucy managed a birthday-girl smile.

Mrs Harris gave her a studied look, but left her to get on.

At the end of afternoon school Mrs Harris clapped her hands for silence.

"Mary tells me you want to hold a meeting," she said, "and I gather I'm not wanted. I don't know what this is all about but here's what I'm going to do. You're all on your honour to behave. Mary is in charge. I'll go off to the staff room for, let's see—" she consulted her wristwatch—"for about ten minutes. That should do. Then I'll come back and see you off home."

She went, closing the door firmly behind her. Mary Gardiner was already at the front, standing behind Mrs Harris's desk.

"Some of us have been talking," she said. "These are our last few weeks in this school. Some of us thought we'd like to give a present to Mrs Harris because she's been so terrific. We wondered if the rest of you would like to join in. Everybody would give money and we would buy something with it. What do you think?"

There was a brief pause while the suggestion sank in. Then, as usual, some of the boys jeered. After that people started chattering all at once, till Mary broke in and made them put their hands up if they wanted to say anything. After that the usual few did all the arguing.

Lucy said nothing. She sat at her table, chin in hands, half listening. She had heard enough about presents for one day.

Samantha came over and sat next to her.

"Don't know how she does it," Sam said. "Nobody would let me hold a meeting."

"Nor me," Lucy said. "Not that I want to."

"Nor me neither," Sam said. "Nobody else could do it," she went on, full of admiration at Mary's command. "There'd be a riot if anybody tried."

"Melanie could," Lucy said.

"Sure," Sam said. "Except she'd do all the talking and we'd have to sit and listen." She gave Lucy a sideways glance. "You certain you aren't being friends?"

Lucy couldn't even be bothered to reply. Sam, rebuffed again, moved back to her own place.

In a way, Lucy thought, Mary and Melanie were two of a kind. Only Melanie used whatever it was they both had to bully and squash people, so they did as she said and hated her for it, while everybody liked Mary (except Melanie and her hangers-on of course) and elected her class leader every time.

It was sickening, Lucy grumbled to herself as the discussion heated up around her, how Mary seemed to know exactly what to do and exactly how to do it, and was good looking as well. If one person in the class could stop Melanie, it was Mary. But of course they both made sure to keep out of each other's way. Almost as if they had a secret agreement.

"Okay," Mary was saying, "I think we've decided that we'll give as much as we want. Anybody who doesn't want to doesn't have to. The present will be from the class, but we'll put in a special card that only those who have given some money will sign. Those in favour put up a hand."

Lucy held up hers because it was obvious you would have to.

"Against," Mary said.

Roland Oliver raised a hand, but he would, just as a joke, Roland having elected himself class comedian. Sally-Ann put hers up too, turned, grinning, expecting to see Melanie's in the air as well, was surprised that it wasn't, and rather sheepishly let her own drop again.

"Only Roland against," Mary said. "Great. There's one more thing. I don't mind collecting the money but I think someone else should buy the present. Any suggestions?"

Silence.

Then Melanie's voice: "Lucy Hall."

Lucy braced, startled out of her dumps. "No!" she called. "I don't want to. Why me?"

Melanie said, "Your dad owns a shop. You'd be good at picking presents."

"Hear, hear!" Gordon James shouted, mocking.

"Good idea," Mary said.

"But—" Lucy spluttered.

Before she could say anything more, Mary asked, "Who agrees?"

A forest of hands. Cheers from the usual boys.

Mrs Harris came in. "Sounds like you've had a good time."

"Thanks, Mrs Harris," Mary said. "We've just finished."

And that was that. They all scattered for home, leaving Lucy trying to gather herself together again.

"See you tomorrow, present picker," Melanie muttered into Lucy's ear as she brushed by on her way to the door.

Lucy wanted to scream.

3

Sarah Hall sat cross-legged on the living-room floor surrounded by a clutter of bills and invoices and cheques and account books. Her fingers flicked over the keys of a pocket calculator lying at her side. The remains of her lunch—scraps of cheese, a bread crust, and an apple core turning brown—lay on a plate behind her.

Stopping in the doorway, Lucy thought: she'll have forgotten the plate is behind her and she'll either sit on it or knock it over. Why does she have to be so untidy? And why does she have to work with her stuff all over the floor?

Sarah glanced up quickly. "Hello, sweetheart. Wishing you'd had a party after all?" Her fingers didn't pause on the keys. Lucy always admired the speed her mother could tap the keys; when she tried it, the calculator went crazy and the answers were billions wrong. "We could still do something to celebrate if you want."

Lucy shook her head. "No. It'll be better in the holidays."

"Can't say I'm sorry," Sarah said. "The VAT man threatens. Got to finish this before supper. Could you make yourself some tea today?"

Lucy nodded.

"Okay at school?"

"Average boring," Lucy said, turning away and crossing the passage into the kitchen.

"Never mind," her mother called, "soon be holidays. Then the High. You'll enjoy that."

Maybe. Weeks away. So who cared? Melanie Prosser was tomorrow.

Lucy had rushed home meaning to talk to her mother about what had happened. Usually she talked to her mother about everything. Sarah was that kind of mum. Which some were not, Lucy knew. A few of her friends came and talked to her mother quite often because they couldn't talk to their own.

But today, when she saw Sarah sitting in the middle of the floor poring over the shop accounts, Lucy felt for the first time that she did not want to talk to her about something important. Not only did she not want to, but could not. It was as if what she wanted to say was too private, even to tell her mother.

Important? Private? Standing in the kitchen surrounded by so many familiar things all higgledy-piggledy as usual, the whole thing seemed silly. Three girls teasing a fourth for a bit of fun. That's what the story would sound like, wouldn't it? Who would take it seriously?

For a few seconds Lucy wondered if the scene behind the cycle shed had really happened. Or at least had been as bad as she remembered. It couldn't have been, could it?

One glance at her wounded shoes and she knew.

But if she told her mother, she'd want to know all the stupid details, all the ridiculous chat. (Sarah was a great one for knowing what everybody said, and as a rule Lucy enjoyed telling her.) And certain sure she would be stomping-mad. She would want to do something drastic about Prosser. Dad would have to be told, and Lucy couldn't bear the thought of his hearing about it. She knew he would feel more hurt than she felt herself—he always was when anything unpleasant happened to her. And this, he would say, was not just unpleasant; it was sordid. Sordid was one of his biggest hate words. And hearing him say it would only make her mother even more agitated.

No, she wouldn't tell them. Interfering parents she could

do without. Anyway, tomorrow might be different. Prosser might only have been trying to scare her today because it was her birthday.

Lucy realized with a start that she had been staring into the cluttered sink for five minutes without moving. She gave herself a glass of iced milk and five Tango biscuits—her favourites but banned at tea time—as a reward and comfort for having survived horrible, rubbishy Prosser, and for keeping her mouth shut, instead of blurting everything all out straightaway to her mum.

On the third biscuit, it occurred to her that, if her mother saw the state of her shoes, keeping her mouth shut would end there and then. Sarah was also a first-rate interrogator. So she flipped the shoes off, stuffed them into her bag, and as coolly as possible made for her room upstairs, clutching her now bulging bag, her half-finished glass of milk and the two remaining biscuits.

With her room door safely shut, she transferred her shoes, after a close, regretful examination of their scars, to a box where she kept old toys hidden at the back of her clothes cupboard.

Looking carefully at her shoes had brought vividly to mind every second of her ordeal behind the cycle shed. Instead of feeling relieved, she felt sick. Sick with Prosser's disease, otherwise known as The Nasties. So far not thought to be deadly. But there was always a first time.

It was as if even her clothes were contaminated. She pulled off her skirt, her blouse, her socks, threw them all into her laundry bag, and put on a favourite red jumper and knock-about jeans and sneakers.

This made her feel a little better; but not knowing what to do next—as if she were standing in a waiting room with nothing to do but wait—she sat on her bed and stared at herself in her mirror. Short hair curling round her head, framing a thin triangular face. A nose she always thought was stubby. Thin long neck. Square shoulders showing bonily through her jumper. Flat chest. Flat, flat chest. How could anybody like her? Even Angus, the steakless wonder?

Lucy stared herself defiantly in her green eyes. "I will not cry," she told herself.

Sarah Hall finished the accounts and sat back onto her plate of leftovers. "Blast!" she said, and cleared up.

Finding no Lucy in the kitchen, she went to the bottom of the stairs and called. A faint and delayed reply.

"Want to help with supper?"

No answer, but sounds of movement.

Lucy wasn't herself, Sarah decided. It wasn't like her to mope. There had been something wrong when she came in. But what?

Sarah went back to the kitchen and set about preparing food.

Lucy arrived looking pale, even perhaps a hint weepy.

"Clean some lettuce?" Sarah suggested.

Lucy stood at the sink where Sarah had dumped a head of lettuce fresh from the garden, its milky juice still oozing from the stem.

Sarah peeled and chopped and mixed.

"No gossip?" she asked when they were well started.

Lucy shrugged. "They did the usual. Some of them gave me cards. Sam gave me a brooch with my name on in Chinese."

"Nice of her. Can I see?"

"It's upstairs." With surprise, Lucy realized she hadn't even bothered to look at it or the cards since she had been given them that morning. Prosser's disease really did things to you.

"Show us when Daddy gets in."

"Okay."

"What are you going to do with the five pounds Uncle Bob sent?"

"Don't know yet."

They worked for a while in silence but for the clack of the kitchen clock. Twenty to five. Sixteen forty!

"Angus Burns gave me another of his silly notes."

Sarah laughed, glad of something to lighten the conversation. "Probably his idea of a present."

"Wants to meet me at the crossing at five."

"How romantic."

"Mum!"

"Well, it is. Crossroads of life. Trains rushing by to exotic places like Swindon. Two beautiful people keeping a secret tryst."

"Yuk!" Lucy was cheering up again. "I'm beautiful, naturally. But Angus Burns . . . !"

"You I'm not so sure about. Angus—I think he's gorgeous."

"You've only seen him once. When you picked me up from school the other day."

Sarah gave her daughter a glancing kiss on the brow as she went by to a cupboard. "Know-all. I've seen him more than that."

"When?"

"In the shop. Buys screws, gardening stuff, tools now and then. Quite the handyman. Can't be for him. For his dad I should think."

"You didn't tell me."

"Didn't think you wanted to know. Always grumbling about how boring he is."

"Well, he is. He's stupid and skinny and all floppy hair, which I'm sure isn't clean, and he's clumsy."

"You wait. In a year or two bumbling Angus will metamorphose into a knockout."

"You do talk rubbish, Mum. And he isn't getting better, he's getting worse. This year he's got really scruffy."

"Have it your own way."

"I don't see how you can tell. Mostly he's just hair and mud anyway."

"Let's say it's something you know when you're me that you still can't know when you're you." Sarah took away the lettuce and plonked a bowl of potatoes and a peeler in their place. "Exercise your fingers on those."

"Do I have to?"

"Do *I* have to?"

"Okay, okay, don't start! What's left for Dad?"

"Washing up the breakfast things, clearing out the waste bin—"

"All right!"

"—bringing in the laundry, plus he wants to mow the lawn because it hasn't been done for five weeks and there are probably elephants lost in it."

"You needn't go on, Mum—I'm sorry I asked."

"Want to help him?"

"No thanks." Lucy jabbed at a potato eye. "Is most of being grown up so boring?"

"Is boring today's word?"

"Forget it."

Ten minutes to five. Sixteen fifty. Could he really have a plan?

"I might as well go and meet Angus if that's okay. I might catch him at it."

"At what?"

"Meta-what-you-said."

"Metamorphosing."

"Could be fun."

"Is he less boring than the spuds?"

"O, Mum!"

"As it's your non-birthday birthday I'll finish them. But don't be long."

"Thanks. I won't. He never has much to say."

"Hello, is that you?" Mrs Prosser shouted from upstairs.

Melanie switched on the television and flopped onto the sofa. "No," she said, "it's the milkman."

Her mother's voice went on, "Your tea's in the kitchen." Then the noise of her clopping feet on the stairs and the smell of her scent coming before her like fog. "You'll be all right, won't you?"

Melanie glanced up. Her mother had tipped the contents of her everyday handbag onto the top of the drinks cabinet and was selecting the few things she wanted in her funbag.

"There's some of your favourite ice-cream in the fridge and a new video I bought specially for you on the table." She stopped sorting and looked across the room at her daughter. "I did tell you, didn't I? I'm meeting your dad after work and we're off to a new club in Bristol. I did say, didn't I, I do remember saying something, and I'm running a bit late. You know how he goes on if I'm late."

Melanie turned back to the television. "Go on, shove off."

Cynthia Prosser grabbed up her funbag, glared at her daughter, said, "Ungrateful brat," and left, slamming the front door behind her, and over-revving the car.

As Lucy strolled up the lane to the railway crossing she saw Angus sitting on the top bar of the gate. A spaghetti-style gnome.

"Thought you weren't coming," he said. "Again."

"I'm only having a walk before supper, so don't excite yourself," Lucy said, stopping in front of him.

An old woman carrying a loaded shopping basket came plodding across the tracks and stood making faces. Lucy nodded towards her, Angus saw at last, and all but fell off the gate. The old woman edged through, eyeing them both suspiciously.

Lucy said, "Are you going to keep me here long? I'm not sure it's safe to be seen with you."

"We could walk along the line. There's some interesting stuff, birds and plants and that."

"I'd rather stay alive, if it's all the same to you."

Angus hitched his jeans and stared sideways across the railway.

Lucy could not understand what her mother was talking about. No sign of any metamorphosing that she could see. He was a head taller than she, which meant he was tall for his age, and he was so slim his grubby blue T-shirt was slack on his body, though this could also be from losing its shape because of needing a good wash. As for his jeans, they might well have no legs inside them for all she could see, except for worn and bony points where his knees must be, one of which, the left, had a hole torn just above it.

Angus glanced at Lucy, aware that she was staring at him. With his right hand he flicked his hair from his face, a habit almost as irritating as his hair hanging there in the first place. But only with his hair pushed back could Lucy see that he had big brown eyes that gave her a shock, they were so unexpected. His hands, however, were long-fingered and filthy, and to hide her surprise she said, "Your dad a coalman?"

"No, why?"

"You look like you've been digging coal."

Angus inspected his hands as if he had never seen them before. "Been planting lettuce," he said, rubbing them down the sides of his jeans, where they had clearly been rubbed many times before. "For my rabbit," he went on. "He works at Daniels."

"Your rabbit works at Daniels?"

Angus grinned. "No. My dad. He's a fitter. On the night shift." He examined his hands again, which on the whole looked worse than before. He stuffed them into his pockets. "Don't see him much. Weekends mostly. He's a bit grumpy sometimes when I get in from school. He's just got up, you see, and sorting himself out for work. He was like that this after, so I put off asking him."

"About the lettuce?"

"About Prosser."

Wary of that name, Lucy said, "What about Prosser?"

"He'll know what to do."

"Angus Burns!" Lucy said, rearing. "Was that your plan? Is that why you dragged me out here to meet you?"

"I thought you were just having a walk."

"What if I don't want you asking your rotten dad about Prosser, or about anything to do with me?"

"He's not rotten and—"

"Maybe I'm going to ask my own dad. Maybe he knows more than your dad about anything you care to mention."

Furious, Lucy was about to stalk off when Angus said, as if reaching a difficult decision, "Yeah, he might."

Lucy swung back, hands on hips. "Who might what?"

"Your dad."

"Just be careful what you say about my dad, Angus Burns!" She wagged a finger at him. "You don't know anything about him. You haven't even met him."

"Yes, I have. In his shop. I often ask him about things I have to buy for my dad. My dad says your dad has the best shop in town for tools and gardening gear and stuff like that and knows about them—"

"O shut up!" Lucy plonked herself down on the grass verge and leaned her back against the fence. The things parents didn't tell you! "I don't want to talk to anybody about Prosser, if you must know," she said. "So I think your plan is a real *futt*."

The warning bell above the gate started clanging, preventing speech with its deafening harshness. The five-nineteen to Gloucester went rattling by. When the bell stopped, the silence itself was a sound for a few seconds.

Melanie picked up the telephone and dialled.

"Hi," she said. "Guess what! Want to come over?"

She listened.

"A new viddy. You'd think she'd left the crown jewels. A rubbishy one as well. Bring one of yours."

More listening. She giggled.

"You aren't half rude!"

She listened again.

"Not till late. After your bedtime anyway."

She laughed.

"See you," she said, and put the receiver down.

"Wasn't going to talk to my dad about *you*," Angus said, sitting an arm's length from Lucy. "If you'd only listen."

"I am listening. Get on with it."

"I wouldn't have said it was you. I'm not that stupid. And I didn't say that was my plan."

"So?"

Angus shuffled. "I was reading this book—"

Lucy chortled. "You—read a book!"

"Why not?"

"What sort of book?"

"A story sort of book, why?"

"You never read books."

"Yes, I do. All the time."

"I've never seen you."

"You're not there all the time."

"When then?"

"In the evenings mostly. After my dad's gone to work."

"Story books?"

Angus rounded on her. "I thought you wanted to know my plan?"

Reading story books—Angus Burns? Lucy stared at him: another surprise. And which books? She was dying to know. But she said, "All right, get on with it."

"In this story," Angus began, and sounding, Lucy thought, as if he were going to tell her every word of it exactly as in the book, "three boys were getting on to another boy—"

"I'm not a boy."

"I know you aren't, but who cares?"

"I do. And I thought you did too, Angus Burns."

"I only meant—"

What Lucy could see of him went red. He turned away, bending his head to look at the ground between his knees, his hair falling like a curtain over his face.

Why don't I keep my big mouth shut, Lucy thought, but said brightly, as if nothing had happened, "Go on, then."

Angus hitched, brushed the curtain open, picked at the hole in his jeans. "The kid they were after kept running and hiding and everything." He paused while he watched a stray scallywag dog pottering by, sniffing at garbage on the other side of the lane.

"And?" Lucy said, nursing her patience. With Angus, she was realizing, you needed lots of patience.

"They kept after him. He kept imagining how he might get rid of them, and his friend wouldn't help, and his mother wouldn't listen, and his dad was away, and there was nobody he could turn to, so in the end—"

"At last!"

"—he decided he just had to stand up to them whatever they did to him, so he and the biggest of the bullies had a punch-up, and the kid got a busted nose, but he hurt the bully as well, and in the story it said how the bully didn't seem as big after that, and didn't bother the kid any more."

Angus glanced at Lucy, waiting for her reaction.

"Yuk!" Lucy said.

Having reached the railway tracks, the litter-hunting dog turned back and came trotting down the lane, paying no attention to Lucy and Angus sitting against the fence.

Angus said, "I haven't told it very good, but the book's okay and funny as well. I'll borrow you it, if you want."

"No, thanks. Are you trying to tell me that your plan is for me to have a fight with Prosser?"

"I'm only suggesting."

"Then don't. Because what you're suggesting, Angus Burns, is that I get myself duffed up. Prosser and Farrant and that creepy Simpson would mince me into little pieces. Look what they do to Clare Tonks."

"They wouldn't if she stood up to them."

"How can she? What could she do?"

"The kid in the story did."

"You and that silly story! It doesn't happen like that. Haven't you noticed? To start with, the big bully probably wouldn't have fought him on his own. The three of them would have got onto the kid all at once. Then where would he be?"

Angus said nothing, but kicked at the grass with a foot. Which, Lucy noticed, wore a running shoe caked in mud and split along the toes.

"He'd have been okay if his friend had helped."

"Nobody helps Clare, or any of the others Prosser goes after. None of my friends helped me."

Angus muttered, "I tried."

"You call that help! And who said you're my friend?"

"Clare Tonks was trying to help."

"Clare Tonks?"

"Yeah, she was standing by the wall and going, 'Don't, don't, you'll only make it worse for Lucy.' And I listened. But she was wrong."

Lucy sniffed. "She was right."

"No, she wasn't." Angus startled Lucy with his sudden anger. "I've been thinking." He stubbed at the grass so hard a tuft went skipping across the lane. "I should have kicked them to death."

Lucy could not help herself feeling pleased at his vehemence on her behalf. "It wouldn't have worked," she said quietly. "They'd only have got you in trouble with Mr Hunt."

Angus pushed himself to his feet. "I hate Prosser," he said. "She's sick."

Above their heads, the warning bell started clanging again. The five forty-four from Gloucester to Swindon.

Lucy got up and brushed herself off while the train clattered by. Angus leaned on the gate, chin on hands, watching it pass.

In the after-silence Lucy said, "They probably won't bother me again."

"Yes, they will," Angus said, not turning round. "And next time I'll pile in."

"No, don't," Lucy said, feeling panic in her stomach. "You won't stop Prosser and everybody will laugh at you. At me as well."

Angus said nothing.

"Do you hear, Angus Burns?"

He turned at last and leaned back against the gate, his hands jammed into his pockets. "Yeah, I hear," he muttered, staring, as far as Lucy could tell, at his feet.

"I've got to go," she said.

The hair nodded.

"Angus Burns," Lucy said, exasperated. "Do me a favour."

"Yeah, what," Angus said, too eagerly pushing the curtain out of his eyes.

"If we have to be friends, at least wash your hair and get it cut. It's *awful*."

Angus, unthinking, put a hand to his head.

"That's right," Lucy said. "The stuff that grows on your noddle."

And she set off down the lane.

Melanie answered the door. She had changed into a pair of tight red jeans and a clingy white T-shirt with ZAP printed across the front in zappy black letters.

"Hi," she said. "Come in quick. There's a right old nosey next door."

"For someone who's boring, you talk a lot about him," Lucy's father said at supper.

"It's just that he's so weird," Lucy said.

"Doesn't seem a bit weird to me," Jack said.

"Nor to me," Sarah said.

Lucy ignored them. "And he's so scruffy. Why doesn't his mother do something about him?"

Sarah laughed. "Why doesn't his dad?"

"His dad works night shift all the time. Angus hardly sees him. Except at weekends. You'd do something about me if I got into the state he's in."

"No," Sarah said. "You'd do something about yourself."

Jack helped himself to more salad. "You must like him or you wouldn't go on so much."

Lucy said, trying to laugh this off, "I do not, Dad. I'm just curious, that's all. Like a scientist who's found a new kind of gruesome maggot."

Sarah and Jack grinned at each other across the table.

As soon as his father had cycled off to work, Angus took the scissors from his mother's workbox and went up to the bathroom. He studied himself in the mirror from as many angles as he could manage. Then he started clipping.

"She sounds a right nurd."

Curling up on the sofa, Melanie said, "She is."

"Just asking for it."

"That lovey-dovey father and that know-all stuckup mother."

"Vomit-making."

"I called her Pukey Lukey this morning. She could have killed me."

"She might try."

"With Farrant around! Farrant's as thick as frozen porridge but she has her uses." Melanie pulled a gormless face and flexed her biceps like a body-builder.

"Hey, that's nice! Do it again."

"Fink!" Melanie said and kicked out.

They both laughed.

"We've got a terrific thing going."

"Tell us, then," Melanie said.

Not altogether sure about his evening's work, Angus checked the doors were locked, that the stove was safely off, found his book, turned off the television, and went to bed, forgetting, as usual, to wash.

Lucy lay in the dark of her room. She could hear her parents two floors below and a background of music playing not quite loudly enough for her to pick out the tune.

She couldn't sleep. Melanie Prosser kept invading her thoughts. She broke out into a cold sweat each time.

Since coming to bed she had been trying to decide what to do. Hope Melanie wouldn't bother her again? Take some small presents and hope that would end it?

Or maybe Angus was right: Prosser wouldn't forget or give up. But what would Prosser do if she didn't take anything tomorrow? Hurt her a bit? Say vile things? Not much else. That was the trouble. Most kids gave in straightaway, just at the thought of what Prosser was supposed to do to you. All because of the stories that went around about her. But take nothing the first time, and more than likely Prosser would find someone else to pick on, wouldn't she?

It was worth a try.

Lucy squirmed onto her back, sighed, and tried to settle down again.

The front door slammed, shutting in arguing voices.

Melanie scrambled to her feet. "Yikes, they're back early!"

She tore round the room, tidying it and herself.

The sitting-room door flew open: Bill Prosser came with it.

"It was lousy!" he was shouting over his shoulder. But was stopped short. "What's all this?" he said, his tone changing to danger. "Who the devil are you?"

"A friend of Mel's."

"Mel's? You mean Melanie, don't you? And who said you could be here at this hour of night?" Bill Prosser glanced at the clock above the fireplace. "Quarter past eleven!"

"O, Dad," Melanie protested.

"Don't O, Dad, me, madam! And you—" Bill said, pointing, "—*out!*"

"We weren't doing anything," Melanie shouted.

"And you—" Bill pointed at his affronted daughter, "—bed. *Now!*"

Melanie stomped from the room, her friend careering ahead of her.

Cynthia Prosser appeared in the doorway. "What are you going on about now, you great lump."

"I hope you've seen to her, that's all," her husband said, marching around the room.

"Stop yelling," Cynthia said, opening the drinks cabinet and pouring herself a large tumblerful.

Melanie's bedroom door slammed, shaking the house.

"You'll have to talk to her," Bill Prosser said, slumping into his chair.

"Talk to her yourself." Cynthia Prosser poured a glass for her husband. "She might listen to you. She doesn't listen to me, that's for sure." She handed him the glass. "Here, swill this down and shut your face."

"And next time," Bill Prosser said, "find somewhere more exciting than that dead hole."

4

Next morning Lucy contrived to be late for school. Sarah was cross with her for not having her things ready. Jack grumbled that she was making him late for the shop. But one way and another she managed to delay leaving the house long enough to be sure that the bell would have gone by the time Jack dropped her off at the school gate. As they arrived, she saw with relief that the playground was deserted.

"Not like you to be late," Mrs Harris said.

"Couldn't find my games things," Lucy said. "Sorry."

She carefully avoided glancing in Melanie's direction, but saw at once that Angus was not in his place. As she settled in her seat, Samantha smiled across at her, repairing yesterday's breach. Lucy smiled back vaguely. Not because she wanted to put Sam off, but because her thoughts, she found to her surprise, were on Angus. Why was he so late?

A few minutes later a note arrived in front of her. She thought for a second that Angus must be there after all and looked quickly round. Only to realize that the note couldn't be his; it was clean and too neatly folded. At once her eyes met Melanie's coolly looking back from her corner table.

Trying not to appear disturbed or much interested, Lucy unfolded the note.

10.30 PENS REST

She had to puzzle at it for a while before she understood what it meant. And then the day closed in, as though she had been shut into a box. Melanie was not going to give up.

Angus arrived at ten past ten. He was wearing his winter anorak with the fur-lined hood up and its draw-strings pulled tight round his face.

"So you've decided to grace us with your presence," Mrs Harris said. "Late even by your standards."

Angus stood by the teacher's desk. There were titters from various parts of the room. Melanie Prosser coughed significantly.

Mrs Harris went on, "It's not raining, is it?"

"No, miss," Angus said.

Warily, knowing Angus of old, Mrs Harris said, "Then why the anorak? And the hood? You'd think we were in January instead of June."

Angus did not reply, just gazed back. Expectant faces waited.

"Well," Mrs Harris said, "take it off and get to work."

"I don't want to, miss."

With heavy patience, Mrs Harris said, "You don't want to take it off, or you don't want to start work?"

"Take it off, miss."

"Whyever not?"

"I've got a note." Angus handed over a crumpled envelope.

Mrs Harris took it gingerly; peered at it, smoothed it out, decided it wouldn't explode, sliced it open with her red pen, and took a page from inside. As Mrs Harris read the letter, Lucy was sure she saw a smile flicker in the corners of the teacher's mouth. But when Mrs Harris looked at Angus again, her mouth was as unsmiling as usual.

"Does Mr Hunt know about this?"

Angus shook his hooded head.

"Never mind now." Mrs Harris folded the letter again and put it into her handbag. "But he'll have to be told. I'll take you to him at playtime."

She surveyed the ear-flapping faces.

"Angus has had a slight accident," she announced in her no-nonsense voice. "You might as well hear about it now so we can get it over. Don't you agree, Angus?"

Angus looked as though Mrs Harris were suggesting she pull out all his teeth with a pair of pliers and no anaesthetic.

"Just remember," Mrs Harris said to them all, "about people who live in glass houses. Anyone—*anyone* can have an accident."

Roland Oliver chuckled. Mrs Harris glared him into silence.

"Now, Angus," she said when she was sure everyone was subdued and ready, "off with that anorak."

Unwillingly, Angus untied the draw-strings, bent forward, and began tugging at the clinging garment. Once it was over his head so that he couldn't see, his hands got tangled in his sleeves. Lucy wanted to rush out and help him, but as it was, Mrs Harris came to his rescue. She took hold of the anorak by the shoulders and with one strong pull emptied Angus out.

There was a moment's suspended pause before everyone, even Mrs Harris, burst into squalls of laughter. Unprotected, Angus forlornly braved the storm.

The accident had happened, of course, to his head. In place of the lank curtain of unruly hair, there was now a dome of short and spiky tufts, looking, Lucy thought, like an old brush that's been chewed by a dog.

But this was not all. From having been a muddy sort of brown, Angus's hair had changed to brightly coloured blotches of various shades of yellow. And the shades ran into each other in a melting sort of pattern.

Once they had taken it in, most of the boys cheered, as if Angus had scored a goal. The girls went on roaring with laughter.

"Looks like a frightened hedgehog!" Priscilla Moulton yelled.

"He's fallen in the Flash!" Sue Dodson shouted.

Angus blinked unhappily at them.

But Lucy all of a sudden was not laughing any more. Angus, she knew now, was not at all what she had thought. He was quite a different person. Her mother was right. Only the metamorphosing hadn't taken a year or two; it seemed to have happened overnight. Now that drooping hair no longer blurred his features she could see his nose and mouth and chin. They were firmly shaped, with clean, neat lines. But what caught her attention most were the eyes. Large, appealing brown eyes she had first caught a proper glimpse of last night at the railway crossing. Now they were glancing here and there, pained with embarrassment. And his embarrassment became hers because she knew why his hair was in such a state.

She wanted to scream at them all to shut up and leave him alone. That it was all her fault.

"It seems," Mrs Harris said at last, quietening the class, "that last night Angus decided to cut his own hair. And as if that wasn't enough, he tried to shampoo it with what turned out to be a sachet of colour rinse. How anyone can possibly manage such a stunning feat of ineptitude, I cannot imagine. But, Angus, if anyone can, you will."

There was more laughter, though of the exhausted kind this time. Laughter for laughter's sake.

Mrs Harris let it blow itself out before saying firmly, "I hope we can all forget Angus's little mishap now, and get back to work. Go and sit down, Angus. Maybe after school this afternoon you'll do something to put right last night's disaster, eh?"

Angus trailed to his place, and fiddled distractedly with his gear, carefully avoiding his friends' eyes. He looked, Lucy thought, on the outside as she felt for him in her inside.

*

The bell went for playtime soon after.

Angus was at once set upon by a chattering, cheering, questioning mob.

In the crush Melanie, Vicky and Sally-Ann hustled Lucy out into the yard, and round behind the cycle shed. Only Clare Tonks paid any heed, and followed.

Meanwhile, Mrs Harris shooed the mob away from Angus, arrested him by the shoulder, and led him off to Mr Hunt's room. A small band of determined and ebullient boys tagged along at a safe distance, only to be waylaid by Mrs Fletcher, patrolling the corridor on duty; she herded them, bleating protests, into the playground.

"*Nothing!*" Melanie's eyes narrowed. "Didn't ask for nothing, Pukey."

"Asked for *presents*," Sally-Ann said, nipping Lucy's thigh so painfully she cried out.

"What's in her bag?" Vicky said, shifting her grip swiftly from an armlock to a half nelson, leaving a hand free to snatch a hank of Lucy's hair.

Sally-Ann tipped Lucy's bag upside down on the ground. The contents spilled at Lucy's feet. She squirmed to break free.

"Wouldn't jump about if I was you," Melanie said. "You'll only tread on your own rubbish." She squatted beside Sally-Ann and the pair of them picked through Lucy's belongings.

"Get your filthy hands off my things!" Lucy cried, struggling against Vicky's grip even though it hurt.

"Shut up, stinky," Vicky growled, yanking at the handful of hair.

Lucy screeched. Tears came, which she couldn't stop. They seemed to have been poised, ready to flow. Anger at their coming added to the insult that was causing them.

At this moment Clare Tonks drifted round the corner.

Lucy tried to hide her face.

"Push off, Tonks," Vicky yelled.

Clare did not budge, but watched from a safe distance.

Melanie glanced up. "Forget her," she said. "She doesn't matter. She'll pay later."

"This pencil sharpener isn't bad," Sally-Ann said, matter-of-fact, as if choosing goods in a shop. "There's a fairly okay key ring with Snoopy on it. And there's a nice felt tip in green. You'd like that, Vick. Green's your colour. And, oooo, look at these, Mel!"

Sally-Ann held up some scraps of scruffy paper. At the sight of them Lucy went wild. She writhed, and tugged, and twisted, and wrenched. She tried to kick; she even tried to bite. But Vicky held on, seeming to enjoy the tussle. Until, panting and trembling with rage, Lucy gave up.

"You haven't had enough practice," Vicky said.

"Beast!" Lucy gasped. "Pig!"

Vicky laughed and gave Lucy's arm a sharp twist that sent pain shooting into her shoulder, making her cry out again.

Melanie said, with mocking pleasure, "They're little love letters from her boyfriend."

"Angus Burns," Sally-Ann said, jigging on her toes. "Yellow mop. Read them out, Mel."

Melanie performed, an actress reading a script: "'Outside the gate after school.' 'You are the greatest.'"

Sally-Ann, peering over Melanie's shoulder, said, "Oooo—kisses!" and swooned dramatically against the wall. "Tell us all about it, Lucy. I bet you had a fab time outside the gate after school. Is that what made his hair shrink and change colour? You must be *dynamite*! All his strength went into snogging. Wasn't an accident at all!"

"Cow!" Lucy shouted.

"Snob!" Sally-Ann yelled, piercingly, back.

"Creep!"

"Smelly, toe-jammy, nitty sow!"

Lucy blustered, but could think just then of nothing really insulting to say.

Vicky muttered into her ear, "You haven't had enough practice at that either."

Melanie said, "Don't know whether he can kiss but he definitely can't spell." She was unfolding the last of the notes. Her face broke into a wide grin. "Listen to this. 'Lucy, beware of Melanie Prosser, she is out to get you. Angus, ex ex ex.'"

"The nerk!" Sally-Ann sneered.

Melanie went on, "'Today seventeen hundred. Railway crossing. Got plan to stop Prosser. Ex ex ex, Angus.'"

"The worm!" Sally-Ann said. "That must be the one he dropped her yesterday."

"What was the plan, Pukey?" Melanie came close up. "Going to blab about us, was he?"

"No, he wasn't," Lucy said. "And I wouldn't tell you anyway."

Melanie tried to outstare her, but couldn't. "Don't matter," she said, turning away. "Hopeless Hunt never does anything anyway."

Sally-Ann performed a twirling dance step. "We say we didn't do it, it's all lies, and he gives up."

"But you'll have to give us extra presents to pay for chatting about us behind our backs," Melanie added.

"Yes," Sally-Ann said. "We'll want really great prezzies tomorrow. Specially as you've brought nothing today."

Lucy said, "I haven't been chatting about you and I won't bring you anything."

"Yes, you will," Melanie said, holding Angus's notes up and waving them under Lucy's nose. "If you want these back."

Sally-Ann giggled. "Otherwise, we might have to stick them up in school for other people to have a good laugh at as well."

"You wouldn't dare!" Lucy exploded with a fresh assault of rage.

"Yes, we would," Melanie said flatly. And she walked away. "Let her go," she ordered without turning when she was well out of range.

Vicky released her grip and she and Sally-Ann ran after Melanie, and all three disappeared round the corner.

Mrs Harris followed Angus out of Mr Hunt's room, closing the door behind her.

"Don't forget what Mr Hunt told you," she said. "That awful hair has to be seen to by tomorrow or you're not to come to school. Tell your father. We can't have a rash of yellow scrubbing brushes among the boys. If you do things like that now, heaven knows what you'll do when you're a few years older. But it won't be my problem, then, thank goodness."

"Yes, miss," Angus muttered, his mind on Lucy and what they might be doing to her. He saw from the school clock that playtime was nearly over. He'd be too late to help.

"And you're to stay in the classroom at dinner time and go straight home after school—"

"But, miss—"

"—I don't want any more scenes like this morning. False heroes I can do without, thank you. Now, go along and catch up with the work you missed. I'll just get my coffee and I'll be there to see to you."

Lucy gathered her scattered belongings and carefully repacked her bag.

Clare Tonks sidled up on feet the size of dinner plates and just as flat.

"You shouldn't let them see you cry," she said.

Lucy sniffed, but did not look up. "What are you on about, Clare?"

"They like it, you see. If you cry they treat you worse."

Lucy stood up, still not able to look Clare in the face.

"Couldn't help it," she said. "They're such—" There wasn't a word bad enough.

"Next time," Clare said, "look at me. It'll help, honest."

Lucy had never had a conversation with Clare before. But she had watched her suffering the same treatment that she herself had just received. She felt guilty about that now.

"Why should looking at you help?" she said.

"Having someone who knows what it's like."

"How do you know there'll be a next time?" Lucy said irritably.

"There will be," Clare said. "You haven't given them anything yet. And them notes—"

"Shut up, Clare. You dare even mention those to anybody—Anyway, I'm not going to give them anything. Rotten thieves."

"They'll go on till you do."

Lucy stared fiercely at her. Tonks the tank. But she still wasn't big enough to stop Melanie. So what could Clare know?

The bell rang for the end of playtime.

Lucy turned away and hurried into school alone.

5

"But it *was* an accident."

Angus had appeared from behind a tree as Lucy walked home. He was encased again in his anorak. Looking, Lucy thought, like a rumpled stick insect. He might be successfully hiding his hair, but he was also making himself more conspicuous in the warm afternoon sun. And if there was anything Lucy disliked, it was being the object of attention from strangers. So she was refusing to stop and talk.

"No one can have an accident like that," she said, not turning to look at Angus and hoping that people in the street wouldn't think they were together. "You wanted to look big in front of the other boys, that's all."

"I didn't. There was these packet things—"

"Sachets."

"—Sachets, and I thought they were all shampoo but they weren't. Some were dyes. Rinses. I dunno. Hair colour stuff."

"Learn to read."

"I can read. I keep saying—it was an accident."

Angus trudged along for a while in silence. Lucy hoped he had given up and would go away. But no.

"It's all your fault," he said morosely.

Lucy stopped in her tracks and swung on him. "What did you say?"

Angus stopped short and took a step back. "You told me to cut my hair and get it washed. I did it for you."

"Don't blame me, Angus Burns, for *that* mess," Lucy said all the more vehemently for knowing she was in the wrong. "I did *not* ask you to cut your hair with the lawn mower and wash it in custard powder."

"If you hadn't of told me, I wouldn't of tried."

"Then please do not do anything I tell you ever again, thanks very much." Lucy swung on her heel and set off once more. All she wanted was to get back to the safe comfort of home, away from beasts like Prosser and apes (even metamorphosing ones) like Angus. She had had enough of everybody for today.

But Angus followed doggedly behind as if towed by an invisible rope. She tried to pretend he wasn't there.

At last, however, by the corner of her own road she could bear it no longer. And she didn't want him following her all the way home, because her mother might ask him in. So she stopped, took a deep breath for patience, and said, "Why don't you go home?"

"I daren't go yet."

"Are you trying to annoy me?"

"No," Angus said with genuine surprise. "I thought after yesterday—"

"What about yesterday?"

"—you know. At the crossing."

With warning in her voice, Lucy said, "What about the crossing?"

"Well—" Angus swallowed. "That we—" He shifted on his feet, watched the traffic, shrugged. "Nothing."

"Then go home," Lucy said.

"I've told you. I *daren't*."

"I'm getting fed up of you."

"It's my dad," Angus said, as though Lucy ought to understand. "When he saw my hair this morning he went mad. I was really scared, honest. He said if I didn't have it right by this after he'd skin me, he'd cut it all off himself. And old Hunt said it wasn't the school's job to see to it and I had to tell my dad to do it. But he'll go wild again, and he always does what he says, my dad, so he will, he'll shave it all off. I'll be bald, honest."

"Don't be silly," Lucy said. "Your mother won't let him."

"How can she stop him?"

"Well, she isn't going to stand there and let your dad make you bald, is she? Mine wouldn't."

For a moment Angus looked suspiciously at Lucy, before he said, "But my mum doesn't live with us."

"O!" Lucy said, and, feeling the need of support, leaned against the corner wall.

"She went," Angus said, "before Christmas. With a friend of my dad's. They used to go fishing together. My dad and him. I thought everybody knew."

Lucy shook her head, unable to think of anything to say.

"It was funny, she didn't take anything, only some of her own stuff in a case. Just went. When I got up in the morning she wasn't there. She'd been okay when I went to bed. She didn't say about going or anything. Just left a letter on the mantelpiece with Dad's name on it. I haven't seen her since. I don't even know where she is. And my dad, he won't say much about it. Says I won't understand."

Angus was talking so quietly now that Lucy could hardly hear him above the noise of the traffic. Suddenly, standing there seemed all wrong. And she was noticing again how much Angus had metamorphosed, and how nicely.

"If you want," she said, "you can come home with me. I expect Mum will know what to do about that hair."

"They're staying in," Melanie said quietly into the telephone, "and some of their twitty friends are coming. They'll be drinking and viddying all night."

She played nervously with the telephone cord while she listened.

"We could go down the park."

Clattering sounds from the kitchen told her she was still safe.

"But why not? . . . I couldn't help last night."

She did not pause for long but her face crumpled at what she heard.

"Just because of that?" she said then, almost shouting. "You know what you are? You're a spotty-faced, horrible creep is what you are!"

She slammed the receiver down, ran upstairs, and locked herself in her room.

Hearing the commotion, Cynthia Prosser flung open the kitchen door and scurried to the bottom of the stairs, steaming saucepan in hand.

"Melanie!" she shouted. "Were you on that phone? You know what your dad said. Stay off it!"

No reply.

"Talk to yourself, Cynthia," she shouted up the stairs, and scurried back into the kitchen, shoving the door closed with her backside and attacking her pans again.

Douglas Burns waited with his bicycle at the garden gate. He had been there ten minutes, looking anxiously up and down the road.

David Waller came along the pavement on his skates.

"Here, Davey," Mr Burns shouted after him.

David freewheeled back.

"Seen our Angus at all?"

"Not since school," David said, wanting to be off.

"Did he seem all right?"

David grinned. "Got a right going over for his hair."

"But you didn't see where he went after school?"

"Ran off Cainscross way. Everybody was ribbing him, but Mrs Harris made him go. She didn't want us talking to him about his hair."

"And you haven't seen him since?"

David shook his head.

"Okay, thanks,"

David scurled away.

Douglas glanced up and down the road again. Thought for a moment. Then swung his bike round, pushed it to the back door, leaned it against the wall, and went inside.

"It'll have to have another rinse later," Sarah Hall said.

"You'll wash my head away soon," Angus said, his voice sounding hollow in the basin, "and I'm whacked."

"Serves you right," Lucy said. She was sitting on the edge of the bathtub, watching.

Sarah said, "Wrap this towel round your head and come downstairs."

They drank Coke in the kitchen while Angus dried out. Sarah snipped at his hair until it was an even length all over.

"They used to call that a crew cut," she said.

Angus looked scrubbed and polished, and his hair was neat and soft and a sunbleached brown instead of custard yellow.

He's metamorphosing even more, Lucy thought, hardly able to take her eyes off him. She smiled to herself but then thought of Angus's notes, which reminded her of Melanie, and of tomorrow, and the inside smile evaporated. She'd die if the notes were put up for everyone to read.

Sarah said, "I think he should keep his hair the colour it is now. Suits him."

"Not bad," Lucy said sipping her Coke.

She and Sarah sat in silence regarding Angus. Then Sarah looked at Lucy, grinned, and said, "Told you."

Lucy smiled back and shrugged, not daring to say anything.

Angus, unaware of what all this meant, said, "My dad probably wouldn't let me keep it like this."

Sarah plonked her scissors down in panic. "O, my goodness! Does he know where you are?"

Angus looked startled. "Dunno."

"The poor man'll be worried to death." Sarah glanced at the kitchen clock. Five forty.

"He'll have gone to work by now," Angus said. "Night shift at Daniels." His face paled, the new-scrubbed bloom gone.

"I'll phone him there," Sarah said. "Just in case."

She was out of the room before they could stop her.

Now that they were alone, Lucy found she couldn't look at Angus. She stared with restless eyes at the crockery littering the table and the wreckage of that morning's breakfast. She heard Angus sniff urgently. She gave him a sideways look; their eyes met and Angus raised his eyebrows as if to say "O, lord!"

From the hall outside they heard the carefully calm sound of Sarah's voice. But she put the phone down much too soon for everything to be all right.

"Apparently," Sarah said when she came back, "he hasn't turned up yet."

They studied one another with closed faces.

"He'll be at home, waiting," Angus said bleakly.

Sarah said, "Lucy's dad has the car. He won't be in till six thirty. I'll walk home with you. It'll be better than phoning."

Resigned, Angus nodded.

Sarah went fussing around the kitchen setting switches on the oven and absent-mindedly moving things from one place to another. Angus dressed himself ready to leave, discarding the towel and pulling on his T-shirt, which looked more drab than ever now that his face and hands were so clean and his hair so trim.

"I'll come too," Lucy said, but knowing.

Sarah shook her head.

"Why not?" Lucy asked, unnecessarily.

"Wouldn't help," Sarah said, a hand on Angus's shoulder to guide him ahead of her. "Daddy will want to know what's happened. While you wait, sort out things for supper, there's a good girl." She paused at the door and gave Lucy a brief kiss. "Won't be long. Best for Angus this way."

They left the house at a busy pace, Angus casting a regretful look back at Lucy, who, watching them go, felt deserted. Jealous for both of them.

"Let me in, you hear me, girl!" Bill Prosser shouted, losing his temper, which never took him long, and hammering on Melanie's door with his fist.

"No!" Melanie yelled back. Apart from the lock, she had wedged a chairback under the door handle.

"I'm telling you, Melanie," Bill Prosser said, "open this blasted door or you'll stay there for the rest of the day."

"Don't care."

From the bottom of the stairs, Cynthia Prosser shouted, "Leave the silly twit. Come and eat your meal."

Bill Prosser fumed.

"She'll come off worst," his wife shouted. "She's the one who'll get nothing."

Her husband rattled at the door handle again. The door shuddered.

"Stupid bitch," he bellowed, and stormed off into his bedroom, slamming the door behind him.

Cynthia Prosser went into the sitting room and poured herself another drink. "One's as bad as the other," she grumbled to herself. "Let them rot, Cynthia."

"Thanks for fetching him," Douglas Burns said.

Sarah said, "No bother. Enjoyed having him. Hope we see him again. 'Bye, Angus."

Angus waved, disconsolately.

When Sarah had gone, Douglas shut the front door. By then Angus was in the living room trying to look normal, and not managing.

Douglas came in and leaned on the corner of the sideboard. Defeated by his father's angry gaze, Angus gave up pretending to be normal, hitched up onto the edge of the sofa, and looked uncertainly across the room at his father.

But the storm didn't burst. Instead, Douglas said quietly, "Might of come home first."

Angus said, shamefaced, "You said I hadn't to till my hair was right."

"Aye well. But couldn't you have gone to the barber's?"

"I tried. Straightaway this morning. I walked all the way into town. But they wanted five pounds twenty just to change the colour. I didn't have more than seventy pence. I had to walk all the way back to school. I was late."

"How late?"

"Ten past ten."

"One mess after another," Douglas said.

"But I did try, Dad."

"You should have asked. I'd have given you enough."

"How could I?"

"What d'you mean, how could you?" Douglas was getting worked up again: the storm perhaps after all. "Are we not speaking or something?"

"After last night?" Angus said weakly.

There was very little between anger and tears.

"Last night," Douglas said, coming to the centre of the room and standing over his son, "I got a bit upset, that's all."

"Worse than before."

"Good heavens, Angus, you'll have to buck up, you know. Life isn't easy. You're growing up now. People aren't always nice to you. You'll have to get used to that."

"It wasn't people. It was you." Angus bit his lip. His breath was catching. "You've never hit me before. I thought—"

His voice choked.

Douglas took a deep breath.

Angus sniffed, wiped his nose on the back of his hand.

"Now then," his father said, quiet again. He took hold of

Angus and, drawing him to his feet, hugged him. "We're both a bit on edge these days."

Neither said anything for a while.

"Not been easy since Christmas," Douglas said at last. They sat together on the sofa.

"Your hair looks better this way." Douglas stroked his hand over it. "One good thing."

"Is she never coming back?" Angus said.

He felt his father go tense. "That's what she says."

"I don't understand."

"No," Douglas said. "It's hard."

"Can't you explain?"

Douglas shook his head. "Another day, maybe. Not today."

There was silence again.

"This morning," Douglas said, "when I saw you with that hair. You reminded me of her."

Angus waited, tense himself now.

"But I shouldn't take it out on you," Douglas said.

Lucy in bed, Sarah and Jack cleared up for the night before settling to watch television.

"She's been in a funny mood the last couple of days," Sarah was saying.

"Maybe it's just her age," Jack said.

"Maybe."

"Angus whatsisname."

"Burns. Nice lad."

"Well then."

"She says she doesn't like him."

"You didn't like me to start with."

Sarah laughed. "Not sure I do yet."

"Thanks!"

"But there's something else. She's moody. That's not like her."

"Growing pains."

They looked at each other, wondering.

"Should we encourage this Angus thing or not?" Jack asked.

Sarah thought before saying, "He's probably just a phase. Bound to happen sometime soon."

"And at least he's bearable."

They smiled at each other.

Their chores done, they switched on the television and sat together to watch.

Lying in bed, Lucy prayed for rain. Rain, she had decided, was her only hope. Preferably with lashings of thunder and lightning as well. And arrange, please, she asked God, for it to happen just before school, during playtime, all through dinner, and again at home time. Then everybody will be kept inside and Prosser won't have a chance.

If He did all that, Lucy promised God, she would not grumble one word, even if she got soaked, just about drowned in fact, all four times, so long as the storms came when required. She wouldn't even grumble at having to do things like helping in the kitchen or cleaning her room on Friday evenings.

And if for some reason known only to God this was not possible, could Prosser please be made to twist her ankle by falling off a wall while showing off on the way to school tomorrow and have to be taken straight back home for a week in bed. And by the way, she added, a wall is not absolutely necessary; anything high enough to fall off will do.

Not that she had found God entirely reliable in the past, she reminded herself, giving up the Almighty as an ally. And there were, now she came to think of it, other ways of getting the better of someone like Melanie. By cunning, for example.

Perhaps she could smarm up to Prosser and offer to share a fizzy lemon drink from her Snoopy vacuum flask.

Tomorrow would be bound to be hot, God deliberately not having provided the required storms as asked, so Prosser would be thirsty. But—ha ha—the lemon fizz would be mostly Andrews liver salts, or some other bog-booster diluted in lemon squash. Prosser, being so greedy, would glug it all down before realizing the fizz was not altogether what it appeared to be. The resulting lurgy would keep Melanie occupied for one day at least; she'd be too busy pooping to bother anybody at all.

But there was also the business of Angus's notes. She'd have to get them away from Prosser somehow. Maybe she could do a trade. A good swig of lemon drink in return for the notes?

Lucy fell asleep rehearsing to herself a satisfying drama in which Melanie took the bait, became bedridden for days on end from weakness because of Lucy's poop bomb, and never bothered anyone ever again.

6

God did not answer Lucy's prayers next day—not the way she wanted Him to at any rate. Nor did she go off to school armed with lethal lemonade. She had not really expected anything better of God, but her own timidity depressed her. And the thought of Melanie letting everybody see Angus's notes was the worst prospect of all.

The day stretched ahead gloomily. As she got out of the car it seemed as if an army of Melanies stood between her and the moment when she would arrive back in the safety of home. She would have given anything to be able to jump back into the car and be driven away to be with her father all day. But the car drove off, Jack giving a cheery wave, leaving Lucy feeling abandoned and helpless at the school gate— a fearful kind of loneliness she had never felt before: a desolation.

Half way up the drive Melanie waited, with Vicky and Sally-Ann on either side, a barrier of bodies blocking her path. Had Lucy known just how awful that day would be, she would have run off home regardless.

"Tie her up," Melanie ordered.

They must have planned it, for they were well prepared. Or maybe they went around prepared all the time. Sally-Ann produced a length of pink ribbon from under her skirt and tied Lucy's hands behind her back, while Vicky held Lucy in a head-lock.

Lucy didn't struggle or call out. There was no use making a fuss. She had decided that from the moment Melanie waved Angus's notes at her as she came through the gate. And anyway, Clare was right: they enjoyed themselves more if you resisted. So let them get on with it, she thought; they would have to stop when the bell went.

This time they had not taken her behind the cycle shed, but stayed openly in the middle of the playground, as if they wanted everyone to see. Which is just what they did want, as it turned out. Clare Tonks hovered about a few paces away, making sure she could see Lucy's face. This time, Lucy stared back at her, and in some unexpected way it did help, like holding hands in the dark, only it was eyes and minds that were being held now.

A small crowd gathered like a ring of spectators at a circus. They knew they were in for some kind of show. "They're yellow," Angus said later. "You weren't kicking up a row so they thought they were safe and they could have some fun watching what Prosser did to you."

But what Melanie did was not what anyone expected.

Angus was not in the playground to watch because he was in Mr Hunt's room having his hair inspected. (He told Lucy afterwards that he was being given a wigging, which Angus thought a great joke.)

Mr Hunt was saying, "I suppose it's an improvement."

Angus did not reply but squinted at the head teacher from under furrowed brows.

Mr Hunt picked through as if looking for nasties. "Is it likely to make further changes overnight," he asked tartly, "or can we hope for time to recover from the shock of this latest hue?"

No reply.

"Well?"

"Don't know, sir."

Mr Hunt wiped his fingers on his handkerchief with elaborate care and sat himself at his desk, regarding Angus with a resigned smile.

From somewhere outside a jeering cheer went up.

"Ladies and gentle-men," Melanie repeated as the cheer that greeted her first show-biz announcement died away. She paraded like a ringmaster. "We 'ave 'ere a speci-woman of that strange and 'orrible h-animile—a Diddicums."

She paused, hand and arm dramatically pointing at Lucy. On cue, the crowd cheered again, as they knew they were meant to. Wasn't it all part of the game?

Melanie went on, "The name of this per-ticlar Diddicums is—Pukey Lukey!"

Most of the crowd laughed; some of the boys gave shrill whistles and clapped.

"This speci-woman, Diddicums Lukey, 'as been captured and brought 'ere at great h-expense for your per-ticlar h-entertainment."

More cheers and clapping. Lucy took a deep breath, as though about to dive under water for a long time, and hung her head. Clare's eyes weren't strong enough to save her any longer.

Melanie, grinning, held up her hands for silence. "But before we see Pukey perform, 'ere with a lyric specially composed for the h-occasion, is the very loverly, the very wonderful, the talented Saucy Songstress—Sally-Ann Simpson."

Louder cheers and shriller whistles and more clapping. The crowd, warmed up now and in the spirit of things, was totally absorbed.

Enter Sally-Ann. She had slipped away behind the cycle shed and made a quick change while Melanie was gathering the crowd; now she appeared in a flouncy pink blouse and slippery wet-look bright red jeans and white tap-dancing shoes.

At the sight of her the cheers became deafening. They

brought Mr Jenkins, the duty teacher, into the yard. He peered over the heads of the spectators. "What's going on?" he asked the nearest girl.

"Some sort of game, sir. They're pretending to give a show."

Mr Jenkins assured himself that nothing untoward was happening, looked at his watch, said, "Not long before the bell anyway," and went back inside.

Sally-Ann, making the most of every second of her big opportunity centre stage, acted the acclaimed star with practised confidence.

Tired at last of applauding, the crowd fell silent.

Sally-Ann waited, smiling sweetly. And at the very second when some impatient spectator might have been tempted to catcall, she suddenly let rip.

Not even Melanie, knowing what was coming, expected such a performance. Some girls in the crowd jumped, and had to ram their hands over their mouths to stop themselves gagging from shock. The usually jeery boys, never having seen anything like it before, were silenced by amazement. None of them could take their eyes from the parcel of irresistible energy that was Sally-Ann Simpson The Saucy Songstress. Only Vicky, standing guard over Lucy, was unaffected. The evening before she had watched Sally-Ann rehearse in the garage of Sally's house.

Sally-Ann not only sang, she also clapped, danced, gyrated like a star from *Top of the Pops*: the showgirl of showgirls.

"*Yeeee-ow!*" she began with ear-splitting force.

"*Yeeee-ow!*" she repeated, pirouetting recklessly.

"*O—yeah!*" she sang.

"*O—yeah!—*Let's hear it now!"

"Let's hear it!" shouted back some of the boys.

And hear it they did, a song-and-dance routine that went:

"This is the story
Of a diddicum girl,
Sweet as sugar—
Keeps her daddy in a whirl.
O—yeah! (two three)—
O—yeah!"
   (*Turn, kick, spin, a quick tap-dance rhythm, clap.*)
"Name of Pukey Lukey—
Jus' look at her smile—
Makes everybody
Want to throw up all the while.
O—yeah! (ain't it right?)
O—yeah!"
   (*Gyrations from Sally-Ann. Loud guffaws from some of
   the crowd. More high kicks, spins, taps, and accompanying
   hand claps from Sally-Ann.*)
"This is how she walks—
I'll show you if you wish.
Nose in the air
And tail out like a fish.
O—yeah! (bump! bump!)
O—yeah! (wanna see?)"
Some of the boys shout, "Go, Sally! Go!"
And now, encouraged by Melanie, almost everyone is
clapping in time.
   "SHALL I DO IT?" Sally-Ann yells.
   "Yes—DO IT! DO IT!" they yell back.
Submitting to popular acclaim, as every great artiste
must, Sally-Ann goosesteps up to Lucy. Stops. Eyes the
crowd. Turns sideways to Lucy. Takes up an exaggerated
posture, nose stuck in the air, chest thrust forward, bottom
poking out backward. Then, keeping to the rhythm of the
clapping, sets off round the circle in a stiff-kneed, waddling
strut that tickles everyone into gales of laughter.
   "O—yeah!" she sings at bellow-pitch as she goes, "O—
yeah!"

She returns again to the centre. Pauses. Makes come-here gestures to the crowd, who, like well-trained dogs, edge closer. And she sings very quietly:

"Tell you what it is
Makes Lukey such a puke.
Got a mammy who's a walker
And a daddy who's a fluke."

Roars of laughter. Through which, breaking into her high-kicking, spinning, tap-dancing, clapping routine again, she sings:

"O—yeah! (That's so)
O—yeah! (Ho ho)
O—yeah! O—yeah!—yeah!
O—o—o—o—yeah . . . ! (Man!)"

The end of the song is greeted with wild cheers, whistles, applause, foot-stomping. Sally-Ann bows, curtsies, does an encore of high kicks for good measure. Would have started again: but Melanie joins her. They bow together. First to one side, then to the other. Then, the deepest bows of all, towards Lucy.

Shouts of "More! More! Sing it again!"

But Melanie walks slowly towards tethered and guarded Lucy.

Instinctively, the crowd know this means a new turn of events, a different excitement. The ovation drains away.

Melanie stops, hands on hips, square in front of Lucy. Only then do most of the crowd notice that tears are running down Lucy's cheeks, and dripping from the end of her chin. The crowd shuffles into a tighter circle, the better to see and hear.

Melanie waits, as Sally-Ann had waited, smiling.

When the crowd is still, she says quietly, "Not clapping, Lukey? Didn't you enjoy it?"

She pauses for an answer. Tears or not, Lucy forces herself to say nothing, nor to make any movement that might suggest a reply.

"Everybody else loved it," Melanie says. And then with sudden understanding, "O, but you've got your hands tied. No wonder you weren't clapping! Untie her hands, Vicky."

Vicky undoes Sally-Ann's tight little knots.

The bell for school goes, but no one pays attention.

Vicky steps back. Lucy's arms fall to her sides.

Melanie says, "Well—go on, Lukey. Now you can clap. You wouldn't like to be *the odd one out*—would you?"

Somehow, in the way Melanie says those few simple words, Lucy hears a terrible message. And when Melanie takes from her jeans pocket Angus's crumpled notes and holds them up, Lucy's will fails. She finds her eyes flicking away, not wanting even to see the scraps of paper. It is as though she is dazzled by a sharp light. Tears come freely and fast now. Her eyes drown; she can see only blurred faces surrounding her. Her thoughts drown too in waves of unhappiness.

"Go on, Pukey," Melanie orders without any pretence of friendliness now. "Clap!"

With torturing shame, Lucy claps.

"They're having a great time out there," Mr Hunt said to Mr Jenkins as he released Angus from his room. "But better call them in."

Mr Jenkins went out into the yard again and bellowed to the crowd, "All right, everybody, let's be having you. Bell's gone."

Angus tried to dodge past, but Mr Jenkins grabbed his arm and hauled him back. "Too late, Burns. Fun's over. Back inside."

In ones and twos the silent crowd broke up and drifted, still silent, into school.

"Gone quiet all of a sudden," Mr Jenkins said as some of his class went by. "Makes a change."

But no one replied. All he got from a few brasher spirits were sheepish grins and quickly averted eyes.

"Too much excitement," Mr Jenkins said. "Not good before school."

Halfway through the morning, sitting distractedly at her work, Lucy felt a nudge and saw a note lying on the table in front of her.

THATS FOR STARTERS
PENS REST TOMORROW OR ELSE

7

That night, in bed, Lucy reviewed her day. Since arriving home she had shut school and Prosser out of her mind. Even Angus as well, who had waylaid her again from behind his tree.

But now, lying in bed with summer evening light still glazing the sky outside her window, everything came sickeningly back.

Her stomach clenched. Though covered only by a sheet, she suddenly felt too hot, and threw the sheet off. Then she felt exposed, defenceless, and pulled it back over her again.

The hot flush turned into a cold sweat. She curled up on her side and tried to lie completely still, hoping this might help her get to sleep. But scraps of her day floated through her mind like flotsam in a stream, the fragments all belonging to one broken object, but jostling by in any old order and swirling away before they could be rescued.

Angus stalking along beside her after school.

"Tomorrow I'll be there. They won't keep me in tomorrow. I'll get there early, really early, and hide somewhere. Just let Prosser start on you!"

Lucy replying desperately, "You can't do anything."

Pens rest tomorrow or else.

Clapping.

*

Mrs Harris checking Lucy's sums. Most of them wrong.

"You don't usually make such silly mistakes, Lucy. It looks like carelessness to me. Were you paying attention?"

And Melanie, moments later, grinning round at the class in a glow of self-satisfaction as Mrs Harris, marking, said, "Very good. Excellent. One thing you do well, Melanie, is your maths."

Lucy standing in a hidden corner behind the school kitchen during dinnertime. How could a warm summer day feel so cold? No one playing with her; but she didn't want anyone.

Clare Tonks plodding into view.

"You shouldn't cry, Lucy. I tried to be where you could see me. But you stopped looking."

Clapping.

Lucy clapping.

Everybody standing silent around her, watching.

And Lucy alone clapping.

Lucy turned from one side to the other.

She could not bear anything like that again, she just knew it.

She could have stood Farrant's stupid pinching and twisting and ridiculous wrestling. And bitchy Simpson's twitting talk. She could even stand Prosser's threats, and mean, jealous, spiteful tricks.

But she could not stand being made a fool of in front of everyone, and hearing them all laugh at idiot things being said about her mother and father. And worst of all she could not stand the thought of Angus's notes on show. It wasn't that Angus had written them, or that they were from a boy—she was secretly pleased at that. It was that they were private. They had nothing to do with anyone else. They were hers. For herself. Not for others to read and say things about. And it was because they were private that everyone would laugh if they were put on show, and make fun of her.

She loathed Melanie for that.

Afternoon school. Sally-Ann flouncing up to Lucy during games on the field, saying, "If you don't bring prezzies tomorrow, Pukey, we'll put your silly notes up, and tell everybody that you go with Angus Burns after school every day and do filthy things in Randwick woods."

Lucy saying, "You dare and I'll kill you, Simpson."

Sally-Ann going on cheerfully, "And I'll tell everybody the reason Angus Burns cut his hair so short is that he's got plaguey nits and the colour is really the stuff they use to kill them."

"You're vile, Simpson."

"Which means, you know, that you've got nits as well, because nobody can do what you two do after school and not catch each other's nits, can they?"

"I'm not listening to you any more, Simpson."

"And besides, Melanie's got something reeeally terrific lined up for you tomorrow, Pukey, you'll see. Reeeally ace. Everybody will be amazed."

Sally-Ann runs off to rejoin her own team.

"We've got to get tough," Angus was saying. "Somebody has to stop her."

"What's this about we, Angus Burns! I'm the only one that's being picked on. And nobody has stopped her yet. Not even teachers."

"Well, somebody ought to stand up to her."

"It shouldn't depend on just one person to stop a gang like Prosser's."

"Then we should gang up on her."

"Sure! You and whose army?"

"A few of us might. Olly and Gordon and Samantha."

"Like today, you mean. Who did they all gang up on today?"

"It wasn't against you."

"It felt like it."

"*They thought Simpson was funny. They were laughing at her. What Prosser did at the end—they didn't like that.*"

"*How do you know?*"

"*We were talking about it this after.*"

"*Talking behind my back?*"

"*No!*"

"*You're on their side now.*"

"*I'm not! I'm just explaining.*"

"*Don't explain to me, Angus Burns. It was me it all happened to, remember? I don't need telling. You weren't even there. How do you know what they were laughing at!*"

"*I was just saying—*"

"*Don't say! All you do is say.*"

"*But I've got a plan—*"

"*And don't tell me about your plans. I know all about your plans, Angus. They're drippy. Stupid. Fliddy. Okay? Now leave me alone. I'm going home.*"

Lucy turned onto her back and shook her head to banish the memory.

Now the sky was dark. The patch of acid orange glow from a street lamp was reflecting on the wall in its usual place.

What might Melanie be planning for tomorrow?

Lucy wished tomorrow would never come. But could not sleep for worrying about what it would bring. Prosser wasn't going to give up, she knew that for sure now. How could she, after today?

Tomorrow was Friday. Get through tomorrow and for two days she wouldn't have to worry about Prosser or any of them. She would be at home. Do what she liked.

She longed for Friday evening to come.

In twenty-four hours she would be lying in her bed, just as she was now, only she would not be feeling so awful. She would lie here and remember tonight, and how she felt now, and know that tomorrow was done with, was over.

Tomorrow would be today and finished. And perhaps by Monday, after two days of not having her to pick on, Melanie would lose interest and get fed up and decide to find a fresh victim.

But tomorrow still had to happen.

Her skin broke out again in a sweat. And inside, her body prickled as though her blood had turned to fizzy bubbles, and her bones were splintering into needles.

No one could help. That was the truth of it. So there was only one thing to do and she would do it.

8

"What've you got?" Melanie demanded next morning.

"Better be something sensational," Sally-Ann said.

"Carbohydrate," Vicky said.

"You what?" Sally-Ann said.

"Carbohydrate," Vicky said. "Got to eat more of it."

"But what is it?"

"Bread and spuds and that."

"Why?"

"Training. Body needs it."

Sally-Ann said to Lucy, "Is that what you've brought—carbonflybait?"

"No," Lucy said.

"Thank goodness," Sally-Ann said.

"Get on with it," Melanie said. The prospect of actually receiving a present at last seemed to make her irritable.

Lucy took an old envelope out of her pocket and handed it over half-heartedly.

Melanie might have been given a filthy handkerchief. "What's this?"

"Having us on." Vicky flexed her muscles.

"Give it here," Sally-Ann said, snatching the envelope from Melanie's disdainful fingers and tearing it open.

Melanie snatched it back before Sally-Ann could look inside. "I'll do it." She fished inside, cautiously, as though it might be contagious, and drew out a five-pound note.

There was a silence.

Then: "Money!" Sally-Ann said flatly as she might have

said "Cabbage" or "Toothpaste" or anything else she thought dull.

"Five quid," Melanie said. "That isn't any good, Pukey."

"O, I dunno—" Vicky started to say.

"Shut it!" Melanie snapped.

Another silence. Melanie crinkled the note between her fingers.

"It's all I've got," Lucy said at last.

Sally-Ann said, "Money doesn't count."

Vicky laughed.

"What's so funny?" Sally-Ann asked sourly.

"Money," Vicky said, "not counting."

"That's funny?"

"Yeah. Counting. Sums. You know."

Sally-Ann ignored her.

Vicky spat at Lucy's feet.

Melanie said, "Money isn't presents. You don't give money to friends." She sounded hurt.

Lucy said, "My uncle sent it for my birthday."

"He must have a really vivid imagination," Sally-Ann said.

"Anyway," Lucy said defiantly, "you're not my friends, and that's all you're going to get."

Sally-Ann went rigid. "You're going to give us some nice prezzies, pig face," she said through clenched teeth, "or next week we're really going to get nasty with you."

She gave Lucy a vicious nip on the arm. Lucy cried out and tried to push away but Vicky grabbed her from behind.

"Twit," Sally-Ann went on, nip-nip. "Noddy. Bean pole. Smelly-nelly." At every word she pinched Lucy again, now on the body, now on the leg, now on the arm, faster and faster. "Squirt. Goofy-creep."

"Stop it!" Lucy cried. "Stop it! Let me alone!"

Tears came again, though she had determined they would not, and shame, and most weakening of all, despair. She was soon sobbing breathlessly as she struggled to break free.

"Let her go," Melanie ordered at last when it seemed that Lucy might become hysterical.

Vicky stood back. Lucy raced away up the path and into school.

"Blubber mouth!" Sally-Ann shouted shrilly after her.

The other two laughed but without amusement.

When Lucy was out of sight, Melanie said, "I'll keep this," and stuffed the five-pound note into her jeans pocket. "Not a proper present, so it's no use to you two, is it."

WANT 2 TALK 2 U

No

Y

Stop sending stupid notes.

Having avoided Angus all day, Lucy was determined not to be ambushed by him after school. She knew if she talked about Prosser and his notes she would not be able to control herself. All she wanted was to be at home on her own. She was starting to hate everybody, not just Prosser and her lot. Except her father; and her mother of course.

As soon as school was over she slipped out of the side gate and walked home the long way round.

Angus waited behind his usual tree. Not having a watch he couldn't tell how long he had been there; but longer than on the other days, he knew. He kept spying round the tree trunk, but still no Lucy.

Then suddenly beside him, having come from a direction he wasn't watching, there was Melanie Prosser.

"Hi, Angus. Been stood up?"

He swung round, scowling. "Push off, Prosser."

Melanie smiled as if Angus were being as friendly as anyone could want. "She won't come now."

"Who won't?"

"You heard what happened this morning?"

"The sun rose."

"Very witty." Melanie enjoyed the joke. "Morning has broken," she sang, mocking Mr Hunt's favourite hymn at assembly. And then said, not able to hide her gloating, "And so has she."

Angus kept quiet, but only with an effort.

"She didn't give us prezzies. You heard? But she did give us this." Melanie fingered in her jeans pocket and pulled out the corner of the five-pound note.

"Liar!" Angus said.

Melanie tossed her hair. "Ask her, then."

Angus stared at Melanie who smoothed her hair and gazed idly down the street, posing herself.

She said, "Mind, I don't care whether you believe me or not. You'll soon find out." She gave Angus a wide smile. "She's just like the rest. Nothing really."

Angus leaned back against the tree.

"Nobody likes being made to look a fool." Melanie was still relishing the memory. "Specially stuckups like her."

"Yesterday, you mean?"

"That was just for starters."

"I don't get you."

Melanie gave him a sly glance. "That'd be telling."

"So?"

"You'd tell her."

"Can't, can I. She isn't speaking."

"But you're still friends."

"Might be." Angus shrugged. "Might not."

"You send her notes. Wait for her here."

"Been spying have you?"

"Watching *you*." Melanie tossed her hair again.

Angus regarded her silently.

"Anyway," Melanie said, "I only tell things to friends."

Angus laughed. "And you haven't many of them."

"Shows what you know, Angus Burns. Only they're not drippos from our crummy school. They're older. From the High actually."

Angus sniffed.

Melanie took the five-pound note from her pocket and crackled it between her fingers. "We could do all sorts with this."

"Like what?"

"Movies."

"Here!"

"Gloucester. It'd pay the fare as well."

"You're full of bright ideas."

"*The Murder of Dracula* is on at the Odeon."

"So?"

"Think I'll go." She gave him a sideways glance. "Want to come?" And she added with a grin, "After all, your girlfriend is paying."

Angus thought a moment. "What about all them friends from the High?"

"What about them?"

"Won't they be jealous?"

Melanie screamed with laughter.

"O well," Angus said, "let them suffer, eh?"

Which sent Melanie into a fresh bout.

"Hey," Angus said, apparently enjoying himself, "reckon I should be on telly."

Lucy stayed in her room most of that evening, listening to her transistor and rearranging her books on their bookcase. They had been in order of the ones she liked most. But from time to time the order changed because she decided she liked others better.

Tomorrow there would have been two more; she had planned to spend some of the money she had given Melanie on new ones. Now there wouldn't be.

She sat on the edge of her bed and stared at her

books till the memory faded.

Last night she had lain in bed thinking that by this time today she would be free from Prosser and feeling happy. But she wasn't; not free or happy. The thought depressed her even more.

She switched off her radio. The noise was replaced by the sound of the vacuum cleaner coming from downstairs. The Friday night house clean. She thought Friday evenings should be for having fun. Going out; enjoying not having school for the next two days. Not for dusting and polishing and tidying. But her parents said that Friday evenings were the only time in the week they could do it.

Tonight though, Lucy somehow found the activity comforting. She went onto the landing and called down.

"Dad."

"Hello?"

"If you fetch the vacuum up, I'll do my room."

"Good heavens! Can this be true? Are my ears deceiving me?" Jack climbed the stairs with the cleaner. "You're not ill, are you?"

Lucy laughed, a relief in itself.

In the interval Melanie bought two ice-creams with the last of Lucy's money.

"You could have a great time," she went on as soon as she sat down again, "with your dad out at work every night."

"You reckon?" Angus slurped his ice-cream.

"I do when mine are out. Which is most nights. My dad's a builder. Has to socialize with his customers."

"Must be loaded."

"Mountains."

"Doesn't pass it on though."

"He does! Whatever I want."

"Why d'you have to take stuff from other kids then?"

Melanie gave him one of her sly glances, and grinned. "Fun, cloth-head."

"Don't seem fun to me."

"Try it and see."

"On Lucy?"

Melanie laughed. "She's starting to bore me. Not that she isn't boring all the time, wouldn't you say?"

"Why bother with her then?"

"Probably won't much longer. Just a couple of times. Till she's got used to the idea. Then you can have a go if you want."

"You're dead generous."

Melanie chuckled. "Big-hearted, that's me."

The lights dimmed. She flipped her empty carton into the air over the heads of the people in front and slunk down in her seat.

Sarah answered the telephone.

"Hello?"

"It's Douglas Burns here, Mrs Hall."

"O, yes, hello, Mr Burns."

"I'm sorry to bother you, but I wondered—have you seen Angus? He's not with you, is he?"

"He isn't, I'm afraid."

"It's just—well, he hasn't come home."

"You mean, not even from school?"

"No."

"Goodness! Just a minute, I'll ask Lucy."

Sarah called upstairs. Lucy came to the banister. "Did you see Angus after school?"

"No, why?"

"But he was in school?"

"Yes. What's the matter?"

Sarah went back to the telephone. Lucy hurried downstairs and sat on the bottom step listening to Sarah's end of the conversation.

"No," Sarah said, "I'm sorry. Lucy didn't see him after school."

"It's not like him to be so late," Douglas said. "Not without telling me. Half past eight."

"Is there anything we can do?"

"No, no. I'll give him a few more minutes, thanks, Mrs Hall, then I'll ring the police."

"Dear me! Seems a bit drastic. Get in touch again if we can help."

Lucy could hardly contain herself. "What's happening? What's he done?"

"Calm down," Sarah said, replacing the receiver. "I thought you didn't like him."

"O, Mum, not that now. What's *happening*?"

"He's late home and his dad's worried, that's all."

"Can't we go looking? He'll be picking stuff for his rabbit or up in the fields playing. He forgets things. Time and things."

"How do you know?"

"I just know. Mum, can't we look?"

"No, no, he'll be all right. He'll turn up, you'll see."

"You're hard, Mum, honest."

"Hard!"

Lucy stomped upstairs to her room.

Sarah watched from below, wondering what on earth had brought on such an outburst. Surely not the news about Angus? Not that alone? Something was upsetting her these days, Sarah could sense it. But whatever it was was something more than first-boy trouble.

Jack, hearing the row, came into the hall. Sarah took him back into the living room to give him the news.

Douglas Burns decided to give Angus till ten o'clock.

Five minutes before the deadline Angus came rushing in, breathless.

"I thought you'd be at work," he panted.

"Never mind where I should be. Where the devil have you been?" Having kept his patience all this time Douglas was seething now as much from relief as from anger.

"Pictures," Angus said, knowing he was for it.

"The pictures! Couldn't you have come home first? Or telephoned even?"

"Couldn't."

"What are you talking about? Couldn't ring your own father? Who were you with?"

"Just somebody."

"Don't you somebody me. Who?"

"You don't know her."

"O, it was a her was it? Is that why you couldn't ring?" Angus nodded.

"Or didn't dare?"

"No, no! It was just—I can't explain."

Douglas laughed dryly. "I'll bet you can't. So who was she? It wasn't the Hall girl, that I know."

"How?"

"Telephoned and asked, that's how."

"O, Dad!"

"Who was it?"

Angus mumbled, "Melanie Prosser."

"Prosser? Prosser the builder? His girl?"

"Suppose."

"You suppose! Must have had a lot to talk about if you didn't find that out. And here—where did you get the money for the pictures? You hadn't enough this morning."

Angus stared at his father speechless.

Douglas couldn't believe it. "You didn't let her pay for you, did you?" He sank heavily into his chair. "I don't know what's got into you lately, Angus. This is the second night this week I've missed work, you know. They'll be sacking me next."

Angus sat on the edge of his chair across the hearth from his father, hugging himself. "I'm sorry, Dad."

Douglas sighed. "I shall have to go on days. It's no good me being on nights. You on your own."

Angus said nothing. He had been wishing his father would make the change, but he knew this was not the moment to say so.

"If they'll wear it," his father went on, "jobs the way they are at present. They'll not be keen."

Douglas and Angus looked at each other. So much to say. But how to say it?

"I nearly had the police out." Douglas smiled.

"You never!"

"Five more minutes."

"Yikes!" Angus went weak at the thought.

"So mind—never again."

Angus shook his head.

"Time you were in bed," Douglas said, standing.

Angus got up, agitated, remembering. "I've just got to ring Lucy—"

"Lucy? Now? This time of night? No you don't!"

"But it's important."

"Rubbish! One girl takes you to the pictures and as soon as you get in you're wanting to ring another."

"But, Dad, it's not like that—"

"Don't care what it's like—bed for you."

"But it's about tomorrow."

"Let's get tonight's fuss over before you start wrecking tomorrow."

"But, Dad, Prosser is going to do something terrible to Lucy tomorrow. I have to warn her."

"Lucy can look after herself. All you've to do is go to bed. NOW."

"But I've got to tell her," Angus shouted.

Exasperated, Douglas took his struggling son by the shoulders and propelled him upstairs, saying, "Enough! I've had all I can stand for one night. You're tired and you're going to bed this second and that's the end of it."

And for Angus, for that night, it was. Douglas stayed home from work to make sure.

9

On Saturday mornings Lucy earned extra pocket money by helping at the shop. While Sarah and Jack looked after customers and staff in the shop itself, Lucy worked in the store room behind, tidying, opening new deliveries, doing whatever odd jobs she was given.

She was there that Saturday morning when Sarah came looking for her.

"There's a girl asking for you," Sarah said.

"For me?"

"She said to tell you it's Melanie."

"Melanie! What does she want?"

"How should I know, sweetheart? The shop's busy so whatever it is, don't hang about in there."

Sarah hurried back to work.

Lucy fumed. How dare Melanie come here? For a second she thought of ignoring her, of letting her wait till she got fed up and went away. But at once Lucy knew this was not a good idea; Melanie would do something embarrassing to attract attention. She might just as well go out and see her, and get rid of her somehow.

It was nine thirty before Angus woke up.

Furious with himself, he ran downstairs to telephone Lucy. No answer, of course.

"O—knickers!" he swore, and scrambled back to his room to dress.

*

"Hi, Lucy," Melanie called in loud friendliness as Lucy approached through the busy shop.

"What do you want?" Lucy kept her voice down and was as unwelcoming as she could be.

But Melanie lost none of her cheeriness. "Thought I'd come and see you, that's all."

"Come outside." Lucy led the way.

Angus had washed and was almost dressed when it occurred to him that Lucy might be at the shop. He almost fell over himself in his rush back to the telephone. But first he had to find the number. This seemed to take decades. Then a hurried woman's voice he did not recognize said, "Handy Hardware."

"Is Lucy there, please?"

"Lucy? Who's this, please?"

"It's Angus Burns. She'll know."

"I'd better get Mr Hall."

"No . . . no!"

But the voice was gone with a clatter of the receiver.

Angus champed. Centuries went by.

"Hello, Angus. This is Lucy's dad."

"Is she there, Mr Hall? It's sort of important."

"She was just now. Hang on."

Clatter again. A millennium passed.

Then: "Sorry. Apparently a friend called for her."

"Who was the friend, Mr Hall?"

"Didn't see, sorry."

"Was it a girl or a boy?"

"Girl I think. We're a bit busy, Angus . . ."

Angus desperately wanted to tell, struggled with himself, took a deep breath to keep it all in. "Thanks," he said, and straightaway decided he would have to cycle into town to find them. He might just be in time.

"What do you want?" Lucy asked when she and

Melanie were away from the shop.

"Nothing."

"Makes a change."

"Just being friendly."

"After this week?"

"O, come on. Just a bit of fun."

"Not for me."

"You shouldn't take things so serious."

"You shouldn't take things."

"Very witty," Melanie said, sharp as a knife. "Like your boyfriend, you mean?"

Lucy stopped and faced Melanie. "What are you on about, Prosser?"

"Hasn't Angus told you?"

"Told me what?"

"We went to the movies last night. Had a *great* time."

"Don't believe you."

"O, but I nearly forgot. *You* paid for the seats, didn't you." Melanie was bubbling with such enthusiastic gratitude that passers-by turned and looked. "*And* for the train fare. Thanks a million, Luce."

She leaned forward and pecked a kiss at Lucy's cheek.

"I still don't believe you," Lucy said, pushing Melanie away but believing every horrifying word. She felt weak from the shock of such betrayal.

"Ask him yourself," Melanie said, and launched into a loud song right there on the pavement, words and movements.

Lucy turned on her heel and set off back to the shop.

"Hey," Melanie called after her, "hang on. What about this morning?"

Lucy marched on doggedly, refusing to answer.

"I haven't had today's prezzie." Melanie might have been pleading.

Lucy stopped dead in her tracks.

Melanie dodged round her, blocking her path. She took

Angus's notes from her jeans pocket and held them up in Lucy's face. "Today," she said encouragingly, "I know what I want."

Lucy sucked in her breath.

"Not money," Melanie went on. "Money's so boring." She grinned. "Well, usually. Not last night though." She waited for Lucy to say something. When she didn't, Melanie pushed the notes at her. "By the way, here's your love letters. You can have them back."

Lucy might have been made of stone. Melanie shrugged and dropped the notes into the gutter.

Lucy watched them fall among the litter of ice-cream wrappers and orange peel and disgusting cigarette ends and used bus tickets. Was that all they were: bits of rubbish to be thrown carelessly away? And was that all she meant to Angus?

The thought of his betrayal drove all the fight out of her. And yet, it was only at this moment, staring at his notes abandoned in the gutter, that she realized how much she liked him.

"Come on, Luce, let's go." Melanie tugged at her sleeve. "After all, he's only a boy! Who cares? You and me can be real friends."

What point was there in resisting? Might as well get it over with. Just as Clare Tonks gave in day after day. Clare Tonks, who Lucy had always thought of as someone pitiful, even ridiculous, for allowing herself to be picked on. But now here she was herself, standing in a busy street outside her own parents' shop, being picked on in just the same way and behaving exactly like poor Clare Tonks.

Poor Clare Tonks? Then poor Lucy Hall. Ridiculous Clare Tonks? Then ridiculous Lucy Hall.

In a mood of deep self-loathing, Lucy said, "Okay, show me."

There was no mistaking the look of triumph on Melanie's face.

*

As Angus stood on his pedals and pumped his bike up Rowcroft hill he saw Melanie, with Lucy trailing after, cross the road ahead and go into Woolworth's.

Sprinting the last stretch, he threw himself off his bike and dumped it beside others against the wall outside, but then got stuck behind a large man and his wife encumbered with loaded shopping bags, and had to follow them slowly into the store. Inside, the crowd was so thick he couldn't see where Melanie and Lucy had gone.

They were standing in front of the music counter. On the wall above was a huge poster of The Pits, top of the charts this week. Oil-smeared skin showing through ripped and tight-fitting garage-mechanics' gear, screaming hair dyed blue, pink and green, the group were swarming over an old banger of a car and threatening the viewer with hammers and spanners, their faces fixed in mocking snarls.

"Aren't they hypnotic!" Melanie was raving. "But I mean *explosive!*"

"No," Lucy said flatly.

"But they're fabulous ace. I could eat them, Luce, honest."

She might too, Lucy thought, from the way she was drooling. This was a Melanie she had never seen before. Not cool, sharp, and in command. But pop-fizzy, just like everybody else.

"I'm dying for their latest album," Melanie said as she scrabbled through cassettes banked on the counter. "Here it is. *Rev, Baby, Rev.*" She turned to Lucy, her fizzy bubble frozen to dry ice. "This is what I want."

Lucy shrugged. "Don't have any money."

Melanie laughed. "You are thick. Don't want you to buy it, Pukey. No fun in that."

Lucy went as cold as Melanie looked.

"It's easy," Melanie said.

Lucy shook her head, her stomach clenching now in panic.

"You'll have to learn sometime." Melanie was as matter-of-fact as if she were explaining a maths problem. "That's the way we get all our best prezzies."

"No," Lucy managed to say.

Melanie chuckled humourlessly. "Got news for you."

"If you want it," Lucy muttered, "you take it."

"Don't be twitty, Puke. Then it wouldn't be a prezzie, would it? And you'd best be quick or somebody is going to start wondering why we're hanging about."

Lucy did not, could not, move.

At which Melanie lost her temper. "Honest, you're so *wet*! There's nothing to it. This time I'll help. But next time you're on your own."

And suddenly, another quick change, Melanie was all smiles and loud talk, giving a performance as a Saturday morning shopper. "O, look, Luce," she sang in a bright honest voice, "there's a new one from Sweet'n'Sour. Aren't they just terrif!" Aside she muttered in Lucy's ear, "Stay close." And all the time her hands were rapidly picking up cassettes and putting them down. "*And* from Charlie Chase. I just loved his last one, didn't you? Ooo, and Hector Protector. I just don't know which to buy. There's too much choice this week. What d'you think, Luce?"

Melanie stopped. Looked back along the counter. Looked round the rest of the store, quite unable to make up her mind, sighed, and said, "Let's go round town while we think about it and come back in a while."

She hooked an arm firmly through Lucy's and guided her with unhurried steps towards the exit. As they threaded through the crowd, Lucy felt something being tucked into the waistband of her jeans.

"What are you doing?" she protested.

"Shut up and keep going," Melanie said, tightening her grip.

(88)

But Lucy used her free hand to remove the object. A cassette of The Pits' album.

They had almost reached the doors. Lucy tried to pull her arm free. Melanie said, "Stop it, stupid nellie!"

And suddenly there was Angus, bursting through the crowd right in front of them, waving his hands.

"Don't go, Lucy," he was saying. "Don't leave, you'll get caught, stay inside."

At once, trembling with rage, Melanie snapped back at him, "Don't you dare, Burns, you pig!"

A laden shopper squeezed by. "Now then, you kids," he said, "go and play outside."

Lucy was confused. What on earth was happening? What was Angus doing here? Why was he flapping his hands about and shouting mad things at her?

But when she opened her mouth to ask, what came out in flat mechanical tones was a quite different question.

"Did you go to the pictures with her last night?"

At which they began shouting at each other all at once.

ANGUS:	LUCY:	MELANIE:
I'll tell you in a minute. But you mustn't leave. Have you taken anything? She said she was going to make you take something. Has she? Have you pinched anything?	If you did, I never want to speak to you again, Angus Burns. You said you wanted to help me and all you've done is make things worse, and now she's trying to make me *steal*.	I'll get you for this, Angus Burns! You just wait! Think you're clever, don't you. But you aren't clever enough. When I start on you, you—you rotten, stinking, brickhead!

It was the word *steal* that ended the row. The sound of it seemed to go off like an explosion around their heads so that everybody must hear it. Though, in fact, no one stopped, or even looked.

But Melanie wasn't waiting to find out. "I'll get you

two," she said, letting go of Lucy's arm. "You wait till Monday!"

And she was gone.

"Have you taken anything?" Angus repeated urgently, paying no attention to Melanie.

"What?" Lucy said, still trying to gather her senses.

"Have you taken anything?"

"No—but—"

"But *what* . . . ?"

"This—" Lucy showed the cassette clasped tightly in her sweating hand. "She stuffed it in my jeans."

"Give it here." Angus snatched it from her.

"What are you doing?"

"Putting it back."

And he was away, weaving through the crowd before Lucy could say anything more. She glimpsed him as he approached the music counter, then her view was blocked by shoppers.

As Angus reached out to put the cassette back a man's hand grabbed his wrist and held it tightly enough to hurt.

"All right, young feller, you'd better come with me."

Angus was swung round, and found himself facing a towering man in shirt sleeves, who might have been any other shopper.

"I was only putting it back," he said, squirming.

"I've heard that one before, old lad," the man said, grinning wryly.

When the music counter came into view again, Lucy could not see Angus.

But then, her heart sinking for she knew what it meant, she saw him being led by a tall, heavy, shirt-sleeved man through a door marked STAFF ONLY.

Later, thinking back over all that happened, Lucy realized this was the moment when she made her decision.

She had had enough of Melanie Prosser. She had had enough of her life being spoiled, of giving in, of doing nothing in the hope that all the nastiness would go away. And she knew she liked Angus enough to be upset if he got hurt, or bothered with another girl, or was in trouble.

She was determined to do something about it. All of it: her own life, and Angus. Starting now.

None of this went through her head then. What she felt was a surge of energy.

She spotted the sales supervisor standing by a check-out and made for her.

"Excuse me," she said in the politest voice she could muster.

"Yes?"

"A friend of mine has just been taken through that door by a man. Could I speak to him, please?"

"O?" The supervisor looked at her closely, suspicion sharpening her eyes.

"All right," the manager said, glowering across his desk while the detective guarded the door. "So you were only putting it back. What proof have you?"

Silence from Angus.

The manager leaned forward. "Do you know that shoplifting is the country's biggest crime? Do you know that stores like this lose millions every year because of it? Do you know it is a crime of epidemic proportions among young people like you?"

Angus shook his head. From the fierceness of the manager's gaze, he felt he himself must have thieved all the millions of pounds' worth of goods and be so contagious he ought to be in an isolation ward.

"If," the manager went on, "*if* you were only putting this cassette back, why did you take it away in the first place?"

"I didn't," Angus said before he had time to think what his answer meant.

But the manager knew and pounced. "So there *was* someone else!"

"No—!" Angus said, fearful now, but realized where this would lead, decided the truth would be best, and added: "Well—yes."

"Ah!" The manager nodded at the detective.

"But she wasn't taking it. Not stealing it, I mean."

"She? The plot thickens." The manager was becoming quite jaunty with success. "Look, lad, I haven't time to mess about. Let's have the truth and get this over. Otherwise, it'll be the police and your parents and maybe even a court case."

Angus felt himself turn sickly white.

The manager's telephone rang. He picked it up crossly. "I'm busy, Peggy, what is it?" As he listened he began to smile. "Is that right? Well, well! Bring her in, will you." He replaced the receiver. "Your accomplice, I gather, young man. Given herself up apparently."

The door opened; Lucy was led in by the supervisor.

Lucy and Angus stared balefully at each other while the three adults, heads together, held a whispered conversation.

When the manager sat down again he said, "Should I expect more of you?"

No answer.

"Well, who's going to begin?"

"It was all my fault," Angus and Lucy said together. Which made them break into giggles; even the detective smiled.

The manager, though, was busy giving Lucy a closer examination. "Aren't you—" he said, searching for a name, "—yes, Jack Hall's girl, what's your name—?"

"Lucy." The giggles vanished.

"Lucy Hall, that's it. Well, well!"

There was a shocked silence. Lucy's mouth went dry.

"Thanks, Mrs Wilson," the manager said to the supervisor. "You get back to the floor. You too, Bill. I'll cope with this. Thanks for your trouble, both."

The supervisor and the detective left the room.

"Now then," the manager said. "I'll have the story straight, please. No frills. Then we'd better get your dad over here, Lucy."

10

They were sitting in the Halls' living room: Lucy, Angus, Douglas, Sarah and Jack.

Everything had come out and been discussed over and over till Lucy was sick of it. Melanie, the bullying, Angus and his hair, Lucy and her birthday money, Angus and the pictures, even Angus's notes, and finally this morning's episode in Woolworth's.

Sarah had taken it hardest. Or at least had said most. Jack had been frostily silent. Which Lucy knew meant he was deeply upset. Douglas was fuming, but restraining himself from saying too much because of the company he was in.

"I knew there was something wrong," Sarah was saying, not for the first time that afternoon. "These last few days you haven't been at all yourself. I wish you'd told me, Lucy."

Lucy, weary, stared at her hands clasped in her lap and kept quiet.

"You can't tell," Angus said, answering for her.

"Usually she tells me everything." Sarah sounded hurt.

"Not this. Only makes it worse," Angus mumbled.

Douglas laughed ruefully. "O, aye," he said, "so this isn't bad enough?"

Jack spoke his first words for more than half an hour. "I know what Angus means. It was the same when we were kids. But something will have to be done."

"You're telling me!" Douglas said. "What those young devils are up to isn't just a bit of bullying. We've all had some of that. It's an organized protection racket. If I had my way, they'd be given a present they'd never forget."

A heavy silence settled on the room.

Then Jack's anger boiled over. "It isn't just presents that that wretched girl is taking from them. Not just *things*. It's now. The present moment. All they've got, damn it! Taking that is the real crime."

He stood up, unable to sit still any longer, paced to the window, looked blindly out, turned, saw four pained faces gazing back at him, and could bear it no more.

"I'm going to make some tea," he said, and left the room.

Half an hour later they were all sitting together again, just as they had been earlier, but calmer now, refreshed by Jack's tea.

Finally Jack hitched himself forward in his chair, put his cup down on the floor, and said in his shop manager's voice, "We can't sit here all day. We'd better decide what's to be done."

Douglas said, "Doesn't that depend a bit on Woolworth's?"

"The manager agreed to wait and see what we can do," Jack said. "Nothing was actually stolen and the kids owned up to what was going on."

"That's a help anyway."

"I suppose I'd better go and see Mr Hunt," Jack said.

Which brought Lucy back to life, protesting loudly. "No, Daddy, no! You'll only make it worse."

Angus too: "He's hopeless! Other parents have tried, honest."

Douglas said, irritably, "Don't be stupid, Angus. He'll have to do something. He'll have to have a go at that Prosser girl for a start."

"He sees her," Angus said, "but she always gets off. There's never any proof."

Sarah burst out: "Well, there's proof this time. There's the two of you. You both know what happened. It isn't just one person's word against another's."

"She'll get out of it somehow," Lucy said.

"I didn't see her take anything," Angus said desperately. "I only stopped them leaving the shop. By then she'd slipped the cassette to Lucy. So that's no proof, is it?"

"You see?" Lucy wailed. "You'll go and see Mr Hunt, he'll make a fuss, but nothing will happen. Except Prosser will pick on me worse than before."

"No she won't," Sarah said. "It might even scare her off."

"It won't! It won't!" Lucy shouted, despairing now, and tears welling up. "You don't understand. It isn't like you think. She gets worse if anybody tells. Like it was a competition between her and the grownups." And the tears flowed. "O, I just wish you'd *listen*. I just wish you'd leave me alone."

She jumped up, fumbling for her handkerchief and, not finding it, ran sobbing from the room.

Sarah stood up to go and comfort her. But Jack said, "Leave her. She'll be better by herself for a minute." Sarah sighed, decided Jack was right, and sat down again.

An awkward silence. They all stared hard at anything except each other.

Then, her turn to lose patience, Sarah erupted: "We can't just sit here while that—that little thug abuses our daughter. Nobody is going to make my daughter's life a misery and turn her into a thief. Not if I can do anything about it. So we've got to do something. I mean it, Jack. I don't care what Lucy says."

Jack leaned towards her, speaking quietly. "But we've got to be careful. Maybe the kids are right. We might make things a lot worse instead of better. In a day or two the Prosser girl will get tired of Lucy and that'll be the end of it."

Sarah was furious by now. "She'll leave Lucy alone and turn her obscene attentions onto some other poor child instead. Is that what you mean? It isn't only Lucy, is it?

She's obviously torturing one girl after another. Well, that's not good enough for me, Jack."

Jack sat back, giving in. He glanced at Angus who was slumped unhappily on the sofa beside Sarah, and thought there was no use in him being put through a row among the adults.

"Angus," Jack said, trying to smile, "why not go up and see how Lucy is?"

Angus, keen to but hesitant, looked at his father, who nodded.

"I don't know where she is."

"In her room, I expect," Jack said. "Up the stairs, top floor, first door."

With Angus gone, the adults relaxed.

Douglas said, "It's the parents I blame. Don't they know what their daughter is up to?"

Sarah said, "Douglas is right, Jack. If they don't know they ought to. And if they do know, it's time they put a stop to it."

"Maybe," Jack said. "But—"

"Never mind the buts," Sarah insisted. "At least if I can't do anything about the school I can do something about the parents. I can go and talk to them. Tell them what's happening. Ask what they're going to do about it."

Jack pulled a doubtful face. "Maybe they know. Maybe there are some parents who couldn't care less what their children get up to. What then?"

But Sarah, adamant, said, "Then they'll just have to be persuaded. At least they should be faced with the problem."

The discussion raged on for another quarter of an hour. But Sarah was stubborn; whatever Jack said, she remained convinced she was right. And with Douglas and Sarah agreeing, Jack had at last to give in.

"I'll telephone and fix to see them tomorrow," Sarah said, feeling much better now there was something to be done, rather than just talked about. "Don't tell the children, it would only worry them. Jack, why don't you take them for a visit to Slimbridge tomorrow while I'm seeing the Prossers? It'll get them out of the way, and they'll enjoy the birds. Take their minds off all this."

Against his better judgement, Jack agreed.

Angus stood outside Lucy's bedroom door and called uncertainly, "Lucy?"

No reply.

"Your dad told me to come up."

Stirrings on a bed. Then Lucy's voice: "Okay, come in if you want."

The room was flooded in late afternoon sun. Lucy was perched uneasily on the edge of her bed, the coverlet rumpled where she had been lying. Her eyes were weepy-red.

Not knowing quite where to put himself, Angus stood awkwardly at the foot of the bed, as if he were visiting someone sick in hospital. But his eyes wandered, curious about Lucy's private things. Her row of big dolls—Paddington Bear, Snoopy, Gonzo Muppet—sitting in a small armchair. Her bookcase with, he guessed, twice as many books as he owned. Her bedside cabinet with its digital clock-lamp on top. Her posters on the wall above the bed, some of animals (a snarling tiger face filled one) and a couple of TV actors to whom Angus took an instant dislike. Her blue wall unit of drawers and clothes cupboard. A long mirror, reflecting himself, ungainly, looking round, and Lucy, watching him from her bed. The whole room neat and trim and bright.

"Better not go into my room," he said, as much for something to say as for any other reason.

"Why?" Lucy asked without enthusiasm, Angus's room not being the most important topic on her mind just then.

"Bit messy." He hitched his jeans.

"I'm made to clean mine up," Lucy said.

"My rabbit's the real trouble," Angus went on.

"Your rabbit?"

Angus nodded. "Clive."

"Clive?"

"He sleeps under my bed."

"You keep your rabbit in your bedroom?"

"Best place. Safe and warm."

"I don't think I'd like that."

Angus shrugged. "He doesn't seem to mind."

Lucy thought it best to change the subject. And there was something else nagging at her she wanted to ask before they went any further. She had to be sure.

"Did you really go with Prosser just to find out what she was going to do to me?"

"I told you."

"But with everybody there. The manager and our parents—Didn't know whether to believe you."

Angus sat cautiously on the corner of the bed. "Look," he said. "I was waiting for you by the tree. She came up. Started wittering on, showing off, boasting. She showed me your five pounds, and said about the pictures. I thought I'd go with her. To find out why she goes on like she does. When we were in the pictures she started hinting about today. I thought if I could find out I could warn you. But when I got back home and was going to ring you, my dad was all worked up and wouldn't let me. And this morning I didn't wake up and you'd gone to the shop and I had to belt off into town to find you." Angus took a breath before adding, "That's all there was."

Lucy observed him closely, making sure before saying, "And you're not friends with her?"

Angus looked at her, aghast. "With her! Yikes, no! I told you, she's sick."

Lucy smiled inside herself. "Still want to be friends with me?"

"Course." Shyness overtook him again. He looked away. "Why did I write them notes?"

"Boys do that."

"I don't. Least, not that sort."

"Do you still like me even though Prosser made me look stupid?" Thinking of the scene in the playground still made Lucy feel tearful.

"Got nothing to do with it."

"Just thought it might have—well, put you off."

"Well, it hasn't," Angus said, leaning elbows on sharp knees and regarding his feet. His short blond hair made his blushes seem all the brighter.

"If you want then," Lucy said quietly, "you can go with me."

Angus nodded.

Lucy waited for some other reply. But as none came, she leaned forward and kissed him quickly, lightly, on the cheek, then sat back hurriedly, cross-legged against the wall.

The red of Angus's blushes deepened, his toes tapped on the floor in a brief little tattoo, he coughed to clear his throat, and nodded again.

Hoping to cover their confusion, Lucy said, "I was glad you turned up in Woolies when you did."

Angus shrugged. "She'll be waiting on Monday," he said. "And she'll be raving mad."

Lucy sighed. "I don't care now," she said, speaking aloud her new determination for the first time, and trembling a little at the sound of her courage. "She's got to be stopped, that's all." Her courage faded a little in the face of itself, and she had to add, "Not that I know how though."

Angus stretched his pencil length across the bed, supporting himself on an elbow. "I've got a sort of idea."

Lucy laughed, as much because of him, as at what he was saying. "Not another of your plans, Angus!"

He smiled and shook his head. "Got it off Clare Tonks."

"Clare Tonks? Why were you talking to her?" Lucy's nervousness for Angus and herself put an edge on her voice.

Angus, knowing, grinned. "She's not that bad when you get to know her," he said.

Lucy, recovering herself, wagged a finger at him. "Angus Burns, you just watch it!"

"I mean to talk to, that's all." They laughed together. "Anyway," Angus went on, "it was her talked to me, really. She said you were the nicest person in our class, and she wanted to help, only you wouldn't let her. She said how if everybody who hated Prosser because of what she'd done to them got together and made a fool of her like she makes fools of them, she would stop picking on other people."

"Did she really say that?"

"Yeah."

"About me, I mean?"

"Yeah. Well, you are really, aren't you? I mean, you're not pushy or anything, like Mary, and you look all right."

"O, thanks!"

"And like Clare said, you're always good at thinking things up."

"Did she say that as well?"

"Yeah."

"Honest?"

"Hope to die."

Lucy indulged in a secret glow of pleasure, but said, "Well, she's wrong about me knowing what to do, isn't she, because I don't."

"But she's right about you having ideas. In drama and when we write stories and that, you're always pretty good."

The secret glow warmed up even more.

Angus sat up, his mind on plans. "You were right. The other day, I mean. About fighting Prosser."

"What about it?" She was always having to jump about in her mind to keep track of him.

"She would. She and her lot."

"Would what?"

"Pulverize you if you tried to fight her."

"So?"

"Even if you did beat her up, I was thinking—that would be just as bad as her beating you up, wouldn't it? It would be bullying her instead of her bullying you. Right?"

"Right." Had she said that? She couldn't remember now. But it didn't matter; Angus was obviously following some track. "Go on, then."

"Well, that means you have to find a way of showing her up, something she hates, but that isn't bad, like beating her up."

"*I* have to?"

"Yeah. Like Clare says, you're good at that sort of thing."

"And what are you going to do?"

"I'll help."

"Thanks!"

"We all will."

"All?"

"Clare and Olly, and Sam and some others. You can do it, Lucy, honest."

Lucy looked at him, his eyes blazing, and laughed. "Talk about Prosser!" she said. "You're even worse."

From downstairs came a shout from Jack. "Angus, your dad's going."

"Rats!" Angus said.

"You can't go now," Lucy wailed.

"I'll have to."

"But we're just getting started."

"I know."

They stared at each other, wishing. But another shout, this time from Douglas, proved they weren't going to be left alone any longer.

Angus opened the door and shouted back, "Coming." Turning, he whispered to Lucy, "You'll think of something. Give us a ring if you do before Monday."

"Okay," Lucy said from her bed, sulky at Angus having to leave.

But when he had closed the door and she heard him clattering down the stairs, she found herself grinning, and hugging herself in a new kind of pleasure.

11

Cynthia Prosser showed Sarah Hall into a sitting room furnished with black vinyl easy chairs and wall units made of chromium steel tubes and smoky glass. All very sharp and bright and Sunday colour-magazine modern. Or at least, Sarah thought, modern as modern had been about ten years ago.

She was not invited to sit down.

"Well," Cynthia Prosser said in a no-nonsense voice, "what about our Melanie?"

Sarah put herself out to be extra polite. "I hope you don't mind me asking, Mrs Prosser, but are you worried about Melanie at all?"

Cynthia flushed. "Worried? Why should I be?"

"She hasn't been in any trouble lately?"

"Trouble?" There was a warning in Cynthia's tone. "What kind of trouble?"

"There's been some bullying at school."

Cynthia went dangerously still, like an animal, Sarah thought, before it strikes.

"My daughter, Lucy, has been a victim of it."

"Has she?"

"Along with a number of other girls, I gather." Sarah struggled to keep her temper. "I wondered whether you had heard anything about it?"

"Can't say I have." Cynthia was straining to sound offhand. "If anybody's been bullying our Melanie, I'm sure she'd have told me."

Sarah knew now there was no hope of a reasonable conversation. "I'm sorry," she said, "but Melanie seems to be the one responsible."

Cynthia Prosser's chin trembled, her lips tightened, a little muscle under one of her eyes flickered. "Just you be careful what you're saying," she said, tight-mouthed, tight-voiced.

Sarah thought: What a hard, hurt woman. And wondered what kind of life was lived in this house. Was it buckled and steely, all glossy surface but hollow inside, like the furniture?

"Melanie and two of her friends have been forcing other girls to bring them presents," Sarah said. "In my daughter's case, Melanie took money as well. And yesterday they went to Woolworth's, where Melanie tried to make Lucy steal a music cassette."

"Rubbish."

"I beg your pardon?"

"Rubbish."

"Are you saying I'm lying?"

"Somebody is. Who did you get all this from?"

"My daughter."

"There you are then."

"Mrs Prosser, are you saying my daughter is lying?"

"Are you saying mine is?"

"Well—"

"Yes, you might well say well! Coming here, accusing our Melanie."

"I've told you, my daughter—"

"Your daughter! She gets caught pinching from Woolies and makes up this cock-and-bull story about Melanie to try and get out of it."

"That's not true!"

"Isn't it? If it's not true, why are you here and not the police? And why hasn't Woolworth's been on to me? Have they been on to you?"

"Of course, that's how it all came out."

"There you are then. Caught red-handed was your daughter, wasn't she, and you believed her pack of lies because you're afraid your prissy reputation might get tarnished. You stuck-up, self-righteous prig!"

"Now just a minute, Mrs Prosser—"

"Get out of my house, d'you hear!" Cynthia Prosser was shouting now. "How dare you come here bad-mouthing my daughter. Put your own child in order first before you preach to other people about theirs. Hypocrite! Go on—scat!"

Sarah, shouted into silence, retreated with as much dignity as her upset emotions would allow.

The Prossers' door slammed behind her.

From upstairs, sitting on the landing outside her room, Melanie heard everything, and smiled with satisfaction.

Her mother's angry face appeared at the bottom of the stairs. "Don't you ever drop me in it like that again. You hear, you stupid cow? And this time I'm telling your father about it."

When Lucy and Jack arrived back from their afternoon at Slimbridge having dropped Angus off at his house, Sarah was still so distraught that she could not help telling them about her visit to Cynthia Prosser.

Lucy was appalled. Melanie really had, like a disease, infected her own home, the one place she had felt was safe, a refuge. Now nowhere was safe any more.

The whole lovely afternoon, the fun she had had with Angus and her father, evaporated, might never have been. The awfulness of the past week flooded back to take its place. And her mother's unconcealed distress became a new oppression.

She sat in the kitchen listening and watching as Jack tried to comfort and reassure Sarah. And even this seemed like another theft, another unwilling present Lucy had to give at Melanie's command.

She was jealous. Jealous of her father for giving such attention to her mother, when it was she, Lucy, who would suffer the consequences of Sarah's foolishness. Why couldn't her father see that? Why didn't he say it?

In the end, Lucy could bear it no longer. With deliberate quietness she got up and went slowly to her room, secretly hoping all the time that her father would call after her, bring her back, console her as he was consoling Sarah.

But he did not; and she closed her bedroom door on the murmur of her parents' voices from the kitchen below.

An hour later, Sarah came into Lucy's room, bearing a tray with beans on toast, a glass of Coke, and three Tango biscuits.

Lucy was huddled in bed, as if from winter cold. Sarah waited for her to sit up and take the peace offering, but she remained determinedly still.

Sarah put the tray down on the bedside cabinet and paused for a moment, hoping her daughter might say the first words. But no. Sarah would have to.

Drawing in her breath, she said, "I've bodged it, haven't I?"

Lucy gave a hint of a nod.

"I'm sorry, sweetheart."

For Lucy to have replied in any way would have meant a deluge of tears. She froze herself against it.

Sarah stood by the bed another moment looking down at her unhappy daughter, then said, with resignation, "Try to eat something," bent, kissed Lucy's cheek, and went back downstairs.

Two hours later Jack came in. By then, feeling hungry, Lucy had eaten the biscuits and drunk the Coke with a rebellious kind of pleasure.

Now she was sitting up reading *Carrie's War* and finding

consolation in it, as well as fellow-feeling. Carrie, the girl in the story, sometimes felt embattled too.

Her father sat by her side on the bed and, smiling, took her hand. "Okay?" he asked.

Lucy nodded.

"Good book?"

"Not bad."

"Want me to read it to you?"

She shook her head.

"Want me to go away?"

She shook her head again. Managed a faint smile.

"Better," Jack said, leaning forward and kissing her brow.

They sat in silence. Outside, dusk was falling. Framed in the window, the sun's last rays haloed the valley top. The room glowed in reflected light.

After a while, Jack said, "It'll pass, you know. It's bad now, but it'll pass."

"But it won't be gone by tomorrow," Lucy said.

"No," Jack sighed. "Can't promise that." After a pause, he added, "Want to stay home for a day or two? Let things blow over."

"No," Lucy said. "I've got to go."

Jack nodded.

Lucy said, "Why are people so awful?"

"Are they? All of them, all the time?"

"Melanie is."

"Maybe you only see her at her worst."

"Why do you always take other people's side?"

"Do I?"

"You're always saying *maybe*. Maybe they didn't mean it. Maybe they couldn't help it. Maybe they weren't feeling well."

"I take your side too."

"But you always do say maybe."

Jack chuckled. "Maybe because I don't believe

anybody is bad all the time."

"Not even Melanie?"

"Not even Melanie, hard though it is to believe."

Lucy was rueful. "She could have fooled me."

"I know. Especially when you're on the receiving end. And I'm not excusing what Melanie has done, you know."

"What are you doing then?"

"Trying to explain. Trying to understand."

"She's rotten, that's all. Angus says she's sick."

"Maybe."

"There!"

They laughed.

"But maybe," Jack said, "well—maybe she's taking out on you something that other people have done to her."

"Like her mother, you mean?"

"Sounds a bit like it from what your mum says."

"Then why doesn't her dad do something? You would if Mum was horrible to me, wouldn't you?"

"Course."

"Well then."

"Maybe—sorry!—but maybe her dad's as bad."

"Or worse."

"Think of that."

"Yuk! I'd rather not."

"We just don't know. That's what I mean, you see? No one ever really knows why someone is bad."

"Not even the person herself?"

"Least of all sometimes."

Lucy thought for a moment. "Still doesn't make it any better."

"No. Not for you this minute. But later maybe."

"Maybe!"

They laughed again.

"Two things you do know though," Jack said.

"What?"

"Stealing won't help."

Glum again, Lucy shook her head. "I won't. I didn't."

"No, I know. But I'm just saying. For the record, eh?"

"What's the second thing?"

Jack smiled. "Something Mum learned the hard way."

Lucy said, "That you and she can't do much to help?"

"Right. Not at present anyway. If there's a solution—"

"I have to find it myself."

"Afraid so."

"I decided that yesterday."

"Told you you knew already."

"Apart from sticking it out till Melanie gets fed up, you mean?"

"Yes. And that's the hard thing I'm having to learn."

"What?"

"That there comes a moment when parents can't always help their children to sort out their lives."

"But you do try," Lucy said with mock generosity.

Jack bowed, smiling. "Thanks, O Queen."

They laughed again.

"Though mind you," Jack said, "talking about it to Mum and me might help. A bit anyway. And we like to know what you're thinking and what's happening to you. Not to pry, but just because we love you."

Lucy looked away, through the window at the fading sky. "Maybe," she said, "I'll just get up for a while and watch TV, if that's okay."

Jack, matter-of-fact, said, "Good idea. Make you sleepy for the night after lazing in bed all evening."

12

On Monday morning Jack drove Lucy up to the school gate as near to starting time as he could manage.

Angus was leaning against the railings as if he had been there all night.

"Sure you don't want me to come in?" Jack said.

"No, thanks," Lucy said, kissing him goodbye.

She got out and joined Angus, and they both waved as Jack drove off.

But Lucy's eyes were already searching for Melanie.

"Hasn't turned up yet," Angus said. "Least, I haven't seen her, and I've been here ages."

"Probably one of her stupid tricks," Lucy said. Having nerved herself for a confrontation, she was on tenterhooks again, once more being made to wait and wonder while Melanie chose the moment.

The bell went.

"I was just ready for her," Angus said, quite disgruntled.

"Me too."

They grinned at each other.

Melanie was not in class by registration either. Sally-Ann and Vicky were there, but subdued without Melanie to direct them. No one knew why she was absent—or rather, no one admitted knowing. But from the way Sally-Ann kept her head down when Mrs Harris asked, Lucy and Angus both decided she did know but was too scared to tell.

With registration over, Mrs Harris set about the day's

work. She suggested that as the end of term this summer was not just the end of the term but the end of their time in this school, they might like to make a wall newspaper. It would be about their lives here—the things they remembered, some of the funnier ones, and some of the sadder ones too perhaps, though Mrs Harris hoped there hadn't been too many sad times. There could be poems, and real-life stories, and drawings. They might even like to bring photographs and include those.

"In fact, it would be the autobiography of your last five years."

"Auto-what, miss?" Brian Webster said, to be awkward.

"*Auto* means self, Brian, as you well know, and biography means—?"

"An account of a person's life," they all called back, except Brian, of course, who was determined to appear as stupid as possible this morning, being Monday, because he knew it tried Mrs Harris's patience.

"Can we do jokes?" Roland Oliver shouted.

"Yes, Roland," Mrs Harris said. "I suppose you can do jokes. Though yours I can usually do without."

General agreement on that score gave Roland considerable pleasure and his friends a chance to cheer.

"What about puzzles and quizzes and that?" Gordon Sims wanted to know.

"The puzzles and quizzes are all right," Mrs Harris said. "I'm not so sure about the *and that*."

"We'll need an editor, miss," Mary said (expecting the job for herself, Lucy thought).

"We will," Mrs Harris said. "But I'll deal with that high office when you've all done your author and artist work."

Mary subsided with as much apparent enthusiasm as she could muster.

"All right, get busy," Mrs Harris said.

There was a general stirring and a lot of chatter at first, while they sorted themselves out, and discussed ideas, and while some of them had a quiet moan at such a soppy idea. But gradually they all got started and even began to enjoy the hard work of writing and drawing rough drafts.

It was during playtime, out in the yard, that Angus brought Clare Tonks over to Lucy.

"Tell her what you just said to me," Angus said to Clare.

Talking to Lucy but looking at Angus, Clare said, "I was wondering what you were doing for the newspaper."

Lucy thought, as she waited for Clare to go on: Why do I always feel she's going to roll over and flatten me to death?

"Because—" Angus prompted.

"Because you might be writing about Prosser."

"Prosser!" Lucy said. "Not likely! I don't even want to talk about her, thanks very much. Why should I write about her?"

Clare said into her chest, "So other people would know."

"Know what?"

"What it's like."

Lucy said, "Write about it yourself then. You know more about what it's like than I do."

Clare stood stock still staring at her feet.

Unable to keep quiet any longer, Angus said, "She will if you will, that's what she wanted to say, and so will I."

Lucy looked at them both, and pretended to laugh this off as a silly idea. But she said to Angus, "Whatever could you write?"

"I could do the biography of a bully, like Mrs Harris said."

"She said do *auto*biography."

"Forget the auto," Angus said dramatically.

"But if you wrote about her, she'd really start on you, wouldn't she? We want to stop her, not make her worse."

"But you don't see what Clare means," Angus said, irritated. "Tell her, Clare."

Clare never said anything much, in class or out, and was

plainly not keen to have a try now. She took a deep breath and let it out loudly. "It's what I tried to tell you before, Lucy. About making fools of people. It's not the nipping and the spitting or that Vicky. Well, they hurt. But they don't matter, not really. It's making fun of you, calling you awful names, and what they say about your mother, and everybody laughing at you. That's the worst—"

She ran out of words; gave Angus a sideways look, appealing for help.

"About laughing at her," Angus said, smiling and nodding encouragement.

Clare even smiled back. "I just thought, if she was made to look a fool, if people laughed at her, she would know what it was like, and that might stop her."

Lucy said nothing. Clare couldn't go on.

Angus said, "She thought you might write something that would make people laugh at Prosser. She says you could do that, but she couldn't."

They looked at each other. Now he had said it briefly like that, the idea no longer sounded convincing. Angus shrugged. "Sorry, Clare. Forget it." And he was turning away to run off and join his friends kicking a football around the field when Lucy said, "No, Angus, wait."

It wasn't so much that Lucy saw now exactly what to do or how to do it, but only that, as Clare and Angus were talking, everything she had worried about and suffered over the last few days, and all her thoughts about how to deal with Melanie, seemed to fall into place. Like a jigsaw puzzle you've stared at for ages that suddenly makes sense, and you realize how the pieces fit together.

For Lucy the important piece that made all the other pieces fit was Angus's notes. Of all that Melanie had done, her threat to display the notes was the worst. Lucy had given money, ashamed of doing so though she had been, just to avoid this happening. And she would have gone on giving presents to stop it, if Melanie hadn't got rid of the notes on Saturday.

Angus's notes would have been on view for everyone to see and laugh at day after day. Everyone would have known; that was the point. Things put in writing for everybody to see were different from things that were only said.

"Clare's right," Lucy said. Clare blinked in surprise. "But it isn't just making them laugh. And it can't be just me. Not just the three of us. That won't stop Prosser. It has to be everybody."

"Everybody!" Angus said, knowing how hopeless that would be to manage.

"Well, not *everybody*, but enough of us who Prosser has bullied to write about what she's done. What she is. And put it all in the newspaper. Then everybody will know."

"They know already," Angus said.

"But not that way. She picks on us one at a time, doesn't she? And no one ever tells, not to us all at once. And we don't ever do anything about her all at once."

"But how is writing about it any different?" Angus said.

"Because nobody has to take her on in a fight that way. It isn't bullying—like you said on Saturday. It's not bullying to write down what's happened to you, is it? Writing it down, I mean, so that everybody can read it. But Prosser would hate it, I just know she would. I would if I was her."

"Me as well," Clare said. She was getting so excited she was weaving back and forth.

Angus said, catching on, "And if Olly did some of his jokes, and Gordon did some of his puzzles, and we get kids from other classes to come and look, Prosser wouldn't hear the last of it, would she?"

"That's what I mean, that's what I meant!" Clare said, and, unable to bear the excitement any longer, had to rush off to the toilet.

The bell went for end of playtime.

"Trouble is," Lucy said as she and Angus walked into school, "none of the others will listen to me."

Angus said, "They'll listen to Mary though."

Lucy nodded and sighed; a problem already.

"We'll just have to get her to join in," Angus said.

Lucy shook her head. "Don't think she would, just for me." And she added a little regretfully, "She might if you asked her with me though."

Angus grinned at her with a glance that betrayed a hint of triumph. "Okay," he said. "We'll grab her in a minute."

They cornered Mary as soon as everyone was settled to work again.

"If it's about Mrs Harris's present," Mary said, "I've got money from nearly everybody now. You could buy it this weekend, I expect."

"It's something else," Angus said, acting as go-between a little too keenly, Lucy felt. "We've got this idea."

"About Melanie," Lucy said, jumping in before Angus could blurt everything out.

"She was rotten to you the other day," Mary said.

"We think she should be stopped," Angus said.

"What he means is," Lucy said quickly, "that it isn't fair what she does. Making fun of people and taking things from kids, and—and—" She could not bring herself to say the word.

"Shoplifting," Angus said straightly.

Mary glanced up to see if Mrs Harris had heard. But she was over at the other side of the room helping Colin Langport who was always needing help.

"What's your idea?" she asked cautiously.

Between them Lucy and Angus explained. "Really show Prosser up," Angus said when they had done.

Mary shook her head. "Don't like it. Naming her, I mean. It would be like telling."

"But why not?" Angus said, indignant. "Why should she get away with it? Look what she's done to stacks of kids this year. And it wouldn't be telling, just describing. That's different."

"If you want to do it, go on, do it," Mary said. "But I won't." She looked at Lucy. "It's a great idea, Lucy, but sorry."

"It won't work without you," Angus said.

"Well, I won't join in if you put names."

"Well, we can't do it without saying who it is, can we?"

Lucy said, "Yes, we can." She had been thinking hard. "It can be a game. We all write about Melanie *without* saying who we mean, but so anybody who thinks about it knows who it must be."

"Puzzles?" Angus said. "Mysteries? Guess-who jokes?"

Lucy nodded.

"Would you go along with that?" Angus said to Mary.

Mary thought a moment, then, smiling, said, "Sure. That would be fun."

By the end of the morning Angus had—without too much difficulty—recruited Roland and Gordon. Lucy had started on her "Guess Who?" biography and had managed to persuade Samantha and Hyacinth Johnson to write something as well because they were friends of hers.

Mary had quietly gone round some of the others who had been on the receiving end of Melanie's attentions and talked them into doing something. She had even had a chat with Mrs Harris and convinced her that part of the newspaper should be what Mary called a "Feature Special" on bullying.

"Sounds depressing to me," Mrs Harris said. "And we don't get much of it here, do we?"

"Not much," Mary said. "But sometimes. And a few of us thought there should be something about it, because it is part of school life, isn't it? Just like in that book you read us last term."

"I remember," Mrs Harris said. "But that was quite funny, wasn't it?"

"Well, we'll be having jokes and puzzles," Mary said, "so

it won't be terrible or anything."

"I should think that would be all right then," Mrs Harris said. "Nothing unpleasant though, and you can be editor of that section, seeing it's your idea."

At the end of the day Mrs Harris said, "We're getting on very well. All sorts of surprises in store. Finish what you're doing for homework, and we'll put the newspaper up tomorrow."

That evening Angus came to Lucy's house after tea and they worked together on their contributions.

They told Sarah and Jack this was secret homework, and that they would show the results later in the week.

Happy that Lucy was more like her old self again, Sarah left them to get on uninterrupted.

There was certainly plenty of laughter coming from the dining room, where they were working. Which, had any of them known it, would be an odd contrast with events at school next day.

13

Extracts from a wall newspaper by Class 4H

??? GUESS WHO ???

She has a habit of biting her finger nails, kicking, pinching, black mailing & pulling hair. *Mary Gardiner*.

?

SHE HAS A GANG. THIS GANG HAS 2 IN IT AS WELL AS HERSELF (=3). THE OTHER 2 ARE VERY FUNNY (U DON'T SAY!!!) AND SILLY-AND-SOPPY (IF U KNOW WHAT I MEAN). *Angus Burns*.

?

She bullies people by making them do her homework and makes you bring presents for her every day and she likes to make you cry. Her hobbies are pulling hair, taking people's things, demanding presents, telling rude lies. She has long dark hair she sometimes chews when she is working. She is clever and good at maths and soon will be twelve and is five feet tall. Lucy Hall.

?

Her hobbies with me are pulling my earings and smashing my glasses. Priscilla Moulton.

?

She comes to school very early and creeps into class and

leaves nasty things in other children's boxes, like spiders and slugs and many other horrible things. She also takes posseshions from other children. *Samantha Ling*.

?

She called me bootpolish and made her gang try to wash me off in the toilet and made some others write stuff on the walls about me which said Go Home. But this is where I live. Hyacinth Johnson.

?

She is tall and I watched her saunter through the playground in her skin tight jeans with her frilly blouse with gold sequins and her wine colour swade boots. Her long brown hair was frizzed (it isn't any more) and she had eye shadow on (which Mr Hunt banned—hate hate). I saw the dominating figure coming towards me. I felt a tug pull me backwards. Her friend had hold of my hair. (I wish my mum wouldn't put ribbons in then maybe she wouldn't notice me.) "Your gonna do my classroom duties, arn't ya." "Yes" I said and with that her friend twisted my arm and all three of them stalked off like chuffed lions. *Maxine Blair*.

?

SHE RUNS AWFULLY FAST AND ITS IMPOSSIBLE TO GET AWAY FROM HER. SHE IS A PERFECT NUSANCE. SHE HAS GREEN EYES A BIG MOUTH AND SHE IS AWFULLY TALL FOR HER AGE. SOMETIMES SHE WEARS A MINISKIRT AND A T SHIRT AND A JACKET AND SOME OF THE LADS WHISTLE AT HER (BUT NOT ME!!) *Gordon Sims*.

?

A Joke (By Roland Oliver, the World's Greatest Comedian)
Q: What did one bully say to the other bully?
A: I get a kick out of you.

FATE
A Puzzle Poem
by Clare Tonks

Many a time I've come to school
Eager for the day ahead. But there,
Leaning on the gate, a bully waits
Alone with her two friends.
No one can ever escape them,
I know that for sure. Then,
Eagerness, like mist, soon vanishes,
Puffed away by fear, when,
Round behind the cycle shed,
Orders are given for your fate:
    "See you've prezzies for us tomorrow,
    See they are just like new,
    Else we'll give you something really nasty.
    Remember, we've got our claws in you."

14

"I said no names!" Mary was brittle with anger.

Angus said, grinning, "It's not names. It's a puzzle."

"Rubbish," Mary said. "Everybody can see. Even Mrs Harris will."

"Tell Clare," Lucy said. "It's her poem. She must have stuck it up after we'd all gone out."

"Anyway," Angus said, "I think it's a terrific poem. Wish I could do something as good."

"Didn't know she had it in her," Lucy said.

Mary was haughty. "She better look out when Prosser sees it, that's all."

"*If* she sees it," Angus said. "She's not back yet."

"Won't work if she doesn't," Lucy said. "Then we'll have wasted all that effort."

Mary, knowing everything, could not help saying, "She fell off her bike. Sally-Ann told me. They kept her home to make sure she's okay."

"Serves her right," Angus said and left them to join his friends who were giggling and pointing at the "Special Feature" in the newspaper, which had a title made by Angus in large letters at the top:

BULLIES.

"Fell off her bike?" Lucy said. She had to sit down; a sudden terrible guilt made her feel weak.

Please, God, she prayed, you didn't did you? I'll never, never, never pray for anyone to fall off anything again, if you'll only make Melanie all right.

She felt dizzy at the prospect that God might actually have been listening all the time. She wondered what else

He might have heard that she would rather He hadn't.

Half an hour later Melanie arrived.

"Good heavens, Melanie, what have you done to yourself?" Mrs Harris exclaimed.

Melanie had a fierce black-and-blue bruise circling one eye and a large dressing plastered over her forehead.

She handed Mrs Harris a letter.

The wall newspaper lost its interest at once, of course; all eyes were fixed on Melanie. There were surreptitious mutterings at the sight of her.

Meanwhile, Mrs Harris shook her head sorrowfully as she read, and then announced briskly: "Melanie met with an accident. But apparently her wounds are only superficial." She inspected Melanie at close quarters. "Though I must say, you do look dreadful, dear."

"I'm all right!" Melanie said sharply enough to make Mrs Harris bridle.

"Are you sure?"

Melanie nodded sheepishly, and, looking away, caught sight of the newspaper, picking out at once, Lucy noticed, Angus's headline: BULLIES. But she turned away pretending not to have seen.

Mrs Harris said, "Very well. But perhaps we'd better let you take things quietly today."

As soon as Melanie was settled in her place, Sally-Ann, perking up, whispered, "Have you seen what they've done?"

"Your name and all," Vicky said. "Need sorting, they do. A few throat chops."

"Wait till you read it," Sally-Ann said with smug satisfaction. "You'll just die."

Melanie ignored them, giving such a good performance of being relaxed, offhand, unaware, that everyone could see she was acting.

"There!" Lucy called to Angus as they sped into the play-ground after lunch. "Making straight for Clare. Told you!"

They ran and caught up just as Melanie said, "You put them up to this, didn't you, fatso!"

"No!" Clare said with a new defiance.

"Liar. And it's your poem, isn't it, and it has my name in."

"Leave her alone," Lucy said pushing between them.

At the same time, Angus was shouting, "Olly, Gordon, Sam, Hyacinth!" and waving them over.

Sally-Ann and Vicky let go of Clare to deal with Lucy. But she struggled, and slipped, and found herself sitting down with a bump. The other two, empty-handed, didn't know what to do, so turned their attentions back to Clare. Which made Lucy realize what an advantage it was being on the ground.

"Sit!" she shouted at Clare, who only stared back, not comprehending. "Sit!" Lucy yelled, sounding as bad as the awful woman on television who barked at dogs.

Obediently, unthinking, Clare sat, plonk, as if her legs had been knocked from under her. Sally-Ann and Vicky fumbled, trying to force her up; but Clare was dead weight, even for Vicky.

"Get up!" Melanie bellowed.

But by now Angus and the others were crowding round, distracting her. She surveyed them in a rapid turn, and forced a grin. "Ganging up, is it," she said.

Angus, seeing what Lucy was up to (or down to) said, "We're not ganging up on anybody, Prosser," and he jack-knifed, sitting cross-legged on the ground. "I'm just watching the show." He looked up at Roland and Sam and the others.

"Yeah," they said, catching on, "yeah, we're just sitting here to watch what you're doing." And they joined Lucy and Angus, sitting on the ground in a circle round Melanie.

Lucy leaned back on her hands, feeling exhilarated at the turn of events: Melanie was not at all comfortable with what was going on. "What were you saying, Melanie dear?" she said.

"Terrific poem, eh?" Angus said. "Clare's I mean."

Sally-Ann screeched, "Go and crawl back down your hole, Burns!"

"Shut it!" Melanie said. "Can't you see what they're trying to do?"

Sally-Ann apparently couldn't: her brow furrowed.

Lucy said, "*We're* not doing anything. You're the one who's doing things."

It was an odd sight: Melanie, Sally-Ann and Vicky standing in a triangle, almost back to back, surrounded by a circle of five or six lounging on the ground. Other kids, curious, came wandering across. "What's on?" they asked. "Another of Mel's shows?" So a second larger crowd was very soon standing round the first. But everyone was unaccustomedly quiet. Nothing seemed to be happening, yet plainly something was. Or was going to.

For a start, no one could mistake that Melanie was seething with fury. Not just angry. But raging. And all her rage was churning inside her like steam locked inside a boiler. The bruise round her eye had turned a vivid, glowing purple; her mouth became a tight, lipless line across her face.

Lucy, sitting in range of Melanie's feet, wondered if she might lose her temper and lash out.

"I'll get you, Tonks!" Melanie said. "Pukey and Burns won't be with you all the time."

"Maybe not, Prosser," Lucy said, "but every time you do anything to one of us, we're going to put something up about it on the wall. We'll keep *notes* about your bullying, and let *everybody* read them."

"Yeah," Angus added, "even if it's just the names of kids you pick on."

After which, to everyone's surprise, Clare said, "And we'll list the presents you take."

"That's right." Lucy said. "A list of names, a list of things you do, and a list of the things you *steal*."

"Where everybody can read them," Angus said.

A silence hung in the air. Melanie looked from one to the next.

Then her rage exploded: the boiler burst, and she screamed with a force that made them all flinch: "You dare! You just dare!"

Her body was rigid, her fists, clenched, beat against her thigh.

Only Angus managed to reply. "Why?" he shouted back. "What'll you do? Take us all on? Make us all shoplift? Not all of us at once, you can't. And we'll be watching. And whatever you do, we'll still write the lists."

Melanie glared at him with deep loathing. "I'll show you if I care about your stupid notes!" she said hissing at him like a cornered animal. "I'll show you what I think of her poem, and your pukey newspaper." She turned, taking them all in. "I'll show you what I think of all you CREEPS!"

And she set off, like a runner from starting blocks, scattering bodies out of her way, sprinting through the crowd and across the playground towards the school door.

Lucy and Angus scrambled to their feet, Clare struggling up after them.

"She's making for our room," Lucy said.

Others had thought of this too and were already racing, first after Melanie, then, realizing they might get stopped inside, swinging towards the windows of 4H's classroom, whose blank eyes were open against the heat.

Lucy and Angus chased after, Clare pounding along behind.

Sally-Ann and Vicky could not at once decide what to do: follow Melanie, stay where they were, or follow the crowd.

But finding themselves alone, hesitated no longer and dashed off after the others.

Lucy, Angus and Clare reached the windows as Melanie came panting into the room. From outside, they watched as she crashed through chairs and against tables, scattering belongings and half-finished work and interrupted books. She made straight for the wall newspaper, reaching out as she got to it, and clawing at Angus's bold headline. She tore at it. BULLIES came ripping down in a streamer of wounded letters. Melanie tore it again and again and again, shredding it into confetti that she scattered around her feet.

Then she reached up again and again in a fever of passion so violent it quite took Lucy's breath away. She ripped and tore and shredded: the Guess Who descriptions, the jokes and puzzles and finally Clare's poem.

Clare's poem sent her into the climax of her fury. She ripped it into smaller and smaller pieces, panting, crying, grunting as she did so.

And then, coming to the window, she tossed the pieces out at Lucy and Angus and Clare on whose heads they fell like ragged snowflakes.

"That's what I care!" she tried to shout, but had no breath for it. "That's what I care!"

And Lucy and Angus and Clare, the rest of the school crowding round, watched with silent, saddened faces.

15

No one saw Melanie again that term. She had been taken for an early holiday, Mrs Harris said; but Sally-Ann babbled about trouble at home with her dad.

"He do poke her in the eye again," Vicky said, laughing.

"Serves her right," Angus said, but felt ashamed.

The Saturday before end of term Lucy and Angus met Mary in town and they chose Mrs Harris's present. Lucy already knew what she wanted to buy but guessed that Mary would like to be consulted.

"What about a set of felt tips for marking?" Lucy said.

"Uses gallons of red on me every day," Angus said.

At the stationer's they picked out three: a red, a green and a black, each with a new kind of tip. They were so cheap there was money left for something else.

"Have you a tray for keeping the pens, please?" Lucy asked.

"How about this?" the assistant said. "There's a place for paper clips, and for an eraser, and the pens rest here."

Lucy and Angus exchanged startled glances.

"That'll be just right," Mary said, taking charge again.

There was a party on the last day. Mrs Harris was delighted with her present. "You've been a pleasure to teach," she said, sniffling.

No one even mentioned Melanie, but Lucy couldn't help remembering. To cheer herself up she looked again at the note clutched in her hand. She had found it a few minutes ago stuck to an ice-cream Angus had brought her.

W8 4 U RLY XING 1630 A xxx